The Blue Lady's Hands

The Blue Lady's Hands

John Champagne

A Mario Sartori Book
Lyle Stuart Inc.   Secaucus, New Jersey

TO ANDREW, AND TO NIC

Published by Lyle Stuart Inc.
120 Enterprise Ave., Secaucus, N.J. 07094
In Canada: Musson Book Company
a division of General Publishing Co. Limited
Don Mills, Ontario

Manufactured in the United States of America

Library of Congress Cataloging-in-Publication Data

Champagne, John.
    The blue lady's hands.

    "A Mario Sartori book."
    I. Title
PS3553.H2647B55   1988   813'.54   88-12310
ISBN 0-8184-0478-7

IF SOMEONE WERE TO ASK ME how I learned what I know about love, I would probably tell them the story of the Blue Lady. She has many other names: The Blessed Virgin, Madonna, Mary. But I have always preferred to call her the Blue Lady. She came to me one night while I was sleeping, and taught me what it means to love someone.

I am not the only one to whom the Blue Lady has appeared; she taught Bernadette how to cure the sick. She told her to mix her spit with dirt, and then wash her face with the mud. Everyone thought poor Bernadette was crazy. But then a spring welled up from the earth, right on the very spot where Bernadette had knelt, scrubbing her skin with dirt. The water from the spring was so pure it healed the sight of a blind man. Afterwards, they made her a saint. I heard all about it in church one Sunday, when I was very young. Only saints get to see the Blue Lady. And she almost never visits men.

In the story of how I learned about love, the Blue Lady appears to me. I wake in the middle of the night to see her standing alongside my bed, her hands resting against my bare chest. At first, I am afraid. She is dressed in robes as blue as a clear sea on a sunny day, and her face is so bright, so radiant, it hurts my eyes to look at her. But then I remember the story of Bernadette, and I am no longer afraid. I realize that I have been waiting for this night all the years of my life.

At first, neither one of us makes a sound. Her hands are counting the beats of my heart, making sure I am ready to learn her secrets. After a few moments have passed, her fingers travel over my chest to the soft space between my lungs. Suddenly, I feel them enter my body, piercing my skin, pushing up beneath my breastbone, up, under my rib cage, past my lungs, and into the chambers of my heart. There is no blood. It is a miracle.

I cry aloud in pain, but make no effort to pull myself free of her hands. Once her fingers enter my heart, she speaks a single sentence. "How much room?" she whispers. Her voice is so soft I can barely hear it, and yet the words are unmistakable. "How much room?"

Before I can ask her what she means, the sky outside my window begins to change. The day begins, and the Blue Lady disappears. I sit upright in my bed, wondering if I have been dreaming. There are no marks on my chest, no cuts or scars, and yet I believe it was not a dream. I know the Blue Lady visited me, and I will never forget her words.

But of course this is all made up. No Blue Lady ever taught me any secrets, and I am certainly not a saint. I invented the whole story once when I fell in love and needed some explanation for the terrible pains in my chest, the feeling of someone's fingers poking around inside me. Sometimes, I wish I had learned about love from the Blue Lady. Even today, when I'm afraid that maybe my heart is too full to make room for anything new, I think of her hands. When I love someone who I don't understand, when I love someone who can't possibly love me back the way I'd like to be loved, I remember her words. "How much room?" And then I wait.

MY MOTHER had a nervous breakdown when I was two years old. She went away to the hospital for thirty-three days (as many as Christ had years). I don't know what went wrong, except that she was depressed. She was only twenty-six. My age now.

Years later, when I was twelve or so, she told me the story of her sickness. Her "cure" was a series of shock treatments administered by her doctor. His nickname was "Electric Louie."

Her illness became a legend to me, my favorite bedtime story. She was the beautiful princess trapped by the evil doctor, who used his machine to make you forget who you were. My father was the hero of the story. He helped my mother escape from Electric Louie and his wicked machine. He saved my mother's life. I saw it written once in a birthday card she'd given him. "Thank you for saving my life so many times."

My father took care of my two younger brothers and me while our mother was away. He rocked us to sleep every night, and we all shared one big bed. I wonder sometimes if the reason I enjoy sleeping with men has something to do with those thirty-three nights of sleeping between my father and brothers.

He was only twenty-eight, with three infant sons, and a sick wife. And he never cheated on her. Ever. That was the burden I carried around with me for the first seventeen years of my life. I expected that some day some man would love me just the way he had loved her. I assumed that one day some man would save me from the sickness I imagined I inherited from her, the sickness that made you hate yourself and feel as if you wanted to die.

I have been in love many times, and always with men. It made perfect sense to me, that I should love men. All my life, everyone has told me how much I am like my mother. Whenever I would tell my father about school, about how much it hurt me when other boys called me "fag" because I hated sports and preferred to act in the school plays, he would always say, "What do you care what other people say? You know, you're just like your mother." When I would stay up all night reading a book, or stay in the house on a sunny day, playing the piano while my father played catch with my brothers, someone—my grandpa, my aunt, my father—would say, "You're just like your mother." My mother loved my father. My father was a man. It only made sense that I should be gay. If I was supposed to love women, my mother would have been a lesbian.

I didn't think that being gay was such a big

deal. I assumed that my life would be just like my parents', except that I would marry a man instead of a woman. I imagined that one day I would meet the man of my dreams, and we would fall madly in love and live happily ever after, just like my parents. And if I ever got sick like my mother, some man would be there to save my life. That is what I thought my life would be like.

But all of that ended the first time I fell in love, when I was seventeen. I learned then that my life wasn't going to be like anyone else's, least of all my parents', no matter how much I wanted it to be so. And now, I am waiting to find out how my life will be. I know I no longer want to be saved by anyone. I don't need saving, and if I did, I could save myself. But I would be lying if I said I am content to live my life alone. I want to learn how to love someone. And I want to be loved by him.

"DON'T SAY A WORD, except that you've never loved anyone the way you love me."

I am speaking to a man I met fifteen minutes earlier. He looks to be several years older than me, probably in his thirties. His black hair is greying at the temples. His eyes look directly into mine for a moment, then dart back down to the page. They are a deep brown color, and surrounded by thick lashes. I wonder how his lashes would feel against my cheek. I recognize his mouth. It is one I've loved before. The lower lip is slightly fuller than the upper, and when he isn't speaking, he looks almost as if he is pouting. It is the kind of mouth I once told a friend reminds me of God in His generous moods.

"I do. I love you very much," he says, once more looking into my eyes. "How could I have survived all those years without you? Kiss me again." He kisses the air loudly, and we both laugh.

It is hot in the city, the kind of night when people roam the streets all night long to try and cool off. A small fan whirs across the room, but I feel no breeze at all. My legs stick to the cushions of an imitation leather sofa. He is seated next to me. His name is Daniel.

I am thinking about dying. Always, on this kind of night, I think about dying. I imagine that I want to die on a night when the heat and humidity are so intense that every single breath is an effort, and your heart beats so strongly you can see your pulse in the tiny veins at your temples. I want to leave the world on this kind of night, when there is no doubt in my mind that I am alive.

We are reading a play. There is the director and there is my friend Jim. And then there is me and the man with the mouth. Daniel.

He smiles at me often as we read. I wonder if he is attracted to me. Maybe he is just being friendly.

The director pours us each a glass of lemonade spiked with gin. He hands us the drinks, telling us when we will rehearse, where we will meet, and how often. I am not listening. I am thinking about him.

What would it be like to touch his thigh? His

arms and legs are covered with thick black hair.

Homosexuals often initiate sexual contact in bars by touching each other's legs.

I read that in a magazine once, years ago, when I was barely a teenager. No one has ever touched my leg who didn't know my name first. Especially not in a gay bar. But I know what that author was trying to say. I feel it whenever another man touches my leg. There is something so unmistakably sexual about the feeling of another man's hand on my leg. I realized it once at a party, when a woman ran her hands along my thighs, and I felt nothing.

I wonder if he has a lover. Or maybe he is one of those men who only sleeps with strangers. I forget about them, sometimes. I forget that no matter how gentle or tender a man may seem, he might prefer anonymous sex to a relationship. I will never understand it. Whenever I meet these men, I think of the Blue Lady's fingers.

Am I attractive? I wonder if I really want to be with anyone. Andrea says yes. I mean, I told Andrea yes. I am paying her thirty dollars a week so that I can learn how to be with a man. Two pitchers of water that spill over into each other and mix. Not an empty vessel waiting for someone else to fill it.

We say good-night. Daniel smiles and looks into my eyes for just a moment, then looks away. After twenty-six years, you would think I'd be able to tell if someone was interested in me. Maybe it's the heat. On nights like this, when it's so hot it's almost impossible to sleep, sex is wonderful. All the liquids of your body pour out like rain, and you feel as if you've just run a four-minute mile. I've never run a four-minute mile. But I can imagine the euphoria and exhaustion. That is what sex feels like on this kind of night. It is sad to be alone in the heat.

Jim and I are walking home. The director? I barely noticed him. I want to talk about Daniel. Should I call and ask him to have dinner with me? Do you think he's attracted to me? "Wait and see," says Jim. "You'll have plenty of time to get to know him once rehearsals begin."

"Does he have a lover?" I ask.

"No, not for a few years. I hear he belongs to a sex club."

"Sex club?"

"Yeah, but it's safe—a jerk-off club. I think he's AIDS paranoid."

Sex club? What would the Blue Lady say about that? I try to imagine Andrea's voice: don't anticipate problems that don't yet exist. Maybe Jim is wrong. Besides, you just met him tonight. Why shouldn't he belong to a jerk-off club? At least it's safe.

And if Daniel and I start to date, maybe he'll stop going to this club. And if we don't date, I am still attractive and there are many available men who want a relationship and I am a good person and not desperate and I don't need to be saved anymore and I AM NOT MY MOTHER.

I wait. The hardest thing to do in the world is to wait and do nothing. But I am going to wait this time.

"Besides," says Jim, "anyone Daniel's age who is *that* nice and *that* attractive and still alone, is bound to be fucked up."

THE FIRST TIME I fell in love, I didn't even have to leave my parents' home. One night, when I was seventeen, a man telephoned me there. A few minutes later, he showed up on their doorstep, and stayed the next few years. More or less. It was just like in the movies. Except that we were both men.

The telephone rang.

"Hello?"

It was a hot summer night, July. I spent many nights that summer waiting to meet the man who was going to love me forever. Mostly, I waited in gay bars. I almost never spoke to anyone I didn't know. I assumed the man who was going to love me would do most of the talking. Getting past the bouncer at the door was never a problem, even though I was a minor. I just changed the birthdate of my driver's license to make me old enough to drink.

"Hello."

My parents knew I went to gay bars. I told them the music was better there. They didn't ask too many questions. At least not right away. I was afraid to tell them the truth, even though I knew I was just like them. Except that I loved men instead of women.

"Hello? Who is this?"

"You don't know me. I got your number from some friends of yours. Can I come over?"

Whoever he was, he was obviously calling from a bar; I could hear disco music playing in the background. I wondered if he had been drinking.

"Why did my friends give you my telephone number?"

"Because I asked them. I wanted to meet you. I've seen you out a few times, and I'd like to get to know you. Can I come over?"

"Is this a joke?"

If he had in fact gotten my number from my friends, then he probably wasn't someone likely to murder me. What could I possibly have been thinking of that night, to invite a complete stranger into my bedroom while my parents slept in the room above? I knew it was only a matter of time before I would meet the man who would love me. Maybe the man on the phone was him. Besides, he said he'd seen me a few times, and wanted to meet me. I imagined myself being watched by a handsome stranger. It sounded so romantic.

"All right, come over. But you have to be quiet because the rest of my family is sleeping. Do you know my address?"

I woke my parents, and told them a friend of mine was coming over. Someone they'd never met. I told them a friend of his had just committed suicide, and he needed to talk to someone about it. I knew they'd understand. Go back to sleep, I told them.

I'd almost never lied to my parents before, and never such a complicated lie as that one. But nothing mattered as much as meeting the right man. Any lie was worth telling if it would help me to find him. This one came out of my mouth as if I'd been planning it for years.

As I heard the sound of his car in the driveway, I ran to the door. I didn't want him ringing the bell and waking up my whole family. Maybe I shouldn't answer it. Maybe he will be stupid, or ugly. No, my friends would have never given him my telephone number. Maybe he will be him. The man who will love me forever.

I opened the door. A man with ash blond hair, eyes the color of blue marble, and a mouth that reminded me of God in His generous moods said "Howdy" and walked into the house. I led him into my bedroom.

He kicked off his shoes and lay across my bed. He wore a blue and green plaid cotton shirt, tan pants, and no socks. I know, because later that night, I wrote down a description of his eyes, his clothes, his mouth. I never wanted to forget that night.

He told me he was twenty-three, an art student on summer break. He told me his name was Michael. He told me he had a lover back at school in the West, a lover of several years. Then, he asked me to sleep with him.

"Tonight?" I asked. "We've only just met."

I tried never to sleep with anyone on the first date. That would be immoral. Sex was only supposed to happen between people who loved each other, or people who thought that some day they might learn to love each other, or people who were trying to love each other. Sex on the first date was not a good idea. Maybe on the second, but never on the first. My parents would never understand.

"Call me tomorrow and we can have dinner."

He kissed me lightly on the mouth and said good-bye. I walked him to his car. I knew that night that I had met my first lover. Or at least I told myself later that I knew it then.

The man who would love me was not supposed to be in love with someone else. And yet it didn't really bother me that Michael already had a lover. Maybe I just wasn't listening.

My parents loved only each other. My mother had never even been with a man before my father. In my plan for meeting the man who would love me forever, there was no room for a third person. But I didn't think of those things at the time. Instead, I thought of Michael's mouth, and how shy he had seemed, even though he'd just asked someone still in high school to sleep with him.

Besides, if Michael and I fell in love, everything would work itself out. His "other" lover would just have to find someone else. Somehow, if it was meant to be, everything would turn out fine. Meanwhile, the lover was off somewhere in the West, while Michael was here with me.

EDITOR'S NOTE: *The following is a letter we received from one of our readers. It is soon to be published in a new anthology of sexually explicit stories.*

I am waiting in the lobby of the theatre for rehearsals to begin. No one else has arrived. I am reading a gay magazine. Not pornography. A "serious" magazine, with news articles, poems, and reviews.

Sometimes, when I'm in search of a little midday action, I head for the third floor restrooms at the Lincoln Center Library for the Performing Arts. On more than one occasion, I've enacted quite a performance there myself.

One afternoon, I happened to be beating my meat while sitting on the toilet. I was in the center stall, hoping someone would come along and give me a hand with my rock hard eight inches. Just as I was about to give up hope, I heard someone enter the stall on my left. Now it was time to make my move.

I wonder what this letter is doing in this magazine. Maybe men who have had to give up anonymous sex because of AIDS are supposed to read it while they masturbate. Maybe it's supposed to prevent them from having unsafe sex. Sublimation for safety's sake, I guess. Or maybe it is just meant to be entertaining.

I slipped my foot beneath the partition, giving the guy in the next stall the signal that I was interested in some hot sex. He responded by touching my foot with his. Quickly, I got to my knees, and stuck my cock beneath the partition. I felt his mouth surround my dick, his tongue licking the shaft like a Popsickle.

I have never had sex in a bathroom. I have

never had sex with someone I didn't know at least by name. I don't understand it. I don't understand why so many men have spent their lives sleeping with strangers. Andrea says it's because straight people have taught us to hate ourselves. She says that "homosexuals" are told that the only way they can express affection for each other is through sex.

But Randy and Brian have been together for years, and they have been with hundreds of men. The Meat Rack on Fire Island, the dunes at Provincetown, the balcony of the Saint, the men's room at Bloomingdale's, at Grand Central Station, at Macy's. Only AIDS has managed to limit their sexual activity.

Randy says I'm too uptight. He says monogamy is the invention of repressed Catholics who hate homosexuals like us. Sex is a sport, meant to be enjoyed. And for all their fights, I know Randy and Brian love each other very much. I've seen Brian lay his head on Randy's chest when they are watching television. I've seen Randy cook Brian's breakfast, preparing his food as carefully as if he were a priest consecrating bread and wine, the body of Christ come down. They will probably be together for the rest of their lives.

After several minutes of heavy duty sucking, I pulled my cock from his mouth. I wanted him to fuck me right there on that bathroom floor. I reached my hand up under the stall. He grabbed it, guiding it to his engorged cock. I stroked his boner, lubing it up with the drops of precum oozing from his head. It wasn't too long—only seven inches—but it was real thick, just the way I like 'em. My asshole twitched in anticipation.

Why am I reading this letter? I get no pleasure from it. Maybe I am trying to teach myself the lesson I can't seem to learn: that everyone has a right to do what he wants with his own body. There is nothing "wrong" with anonymous sex. Maybe I am punishing myself because I will never believe that fucking strangers in public bathrooms is "fun" or "hot."

I am not my parents, but this letter has nothing to do with my life. That is the joke the Blue Lady plays on me. She shows me that no matter who I'm with, I can never quite manage to fit in. Not with straight people. Not with gay men. Why is loving men so painful?

Nothing human disgusts me. Andrea reminds me over and over again of these words she says are Oscar Wilde's. But these men, they don't disgust me. I feel for them. If I could, I would protect them from this ugliness. I want to hold them, to protect them. I wonder who has hurt them so much that they can no longer bear to be loved.

But what right have I to make judgments about other people's sex lives? Maybe if it weren't for AIDS, I'd be sleeping with strangers too. Maybe if it weren't for my parents, I'd be fucking in bathrooms. Sex isn't love. I know that.

The door of the lobby swings open. "Hi, how are you?" asks Daniel. He smiles at me.

THERE IS a brown corduroy sofa on which I've never sat, and a rectangular pink coffee table made of marble. A box of tissues always sits atop the table. I wonder if all psychiatrists' offices come equipped with a box of tissues.

Two wooden chairs flank the table, one on either side. I always take the one nearest the door. Andrea sits in the chair opposite mine.

"So, how are things going?" she asks.

For three years now, we have been spending one hour a week talking about my life. I feel sometimes as if I've told her everything, every second I've ever lived. I wonder sometimes when I will be "done." We've never spoken about stopping. I guess I'm supposed to decide when it will be over. In my own mind, I have already decided. Therapy will end once I am "successfully involved in a significant relationship."

It's not that I believe that being in love will end all my problems. But nothing seems to be as difficult as learning how to love someone. It is the one part of my life that I don't think I can handle all by myself.

I want to love someone in a good way. No obsessions, no being saved, no "I need you so much I can't live without you." Where do I learn? I am not my parents. But I am also not Randy and Brian.

I tell Andrea about Daniel, how he smiles, how nice he seems, how I'd like to ask him out.

"How long have you known him?"

Three weeks? Four weeks. I tell her about

rehearsals, the way he holds my gaze for just a moment, then looks away. And once, when my script fell, he touched my hand as we gathered up the pages.

"Go ahead and ask him. But try not to be too intense about it. Don't pressure him if he seems reluctant."

Oh God, what if, Don't be too intense, she said, it's only a date, and he's not the very last person on earth, and there is no one "right" man for you, and you are not your parents. Take it slowly; you are not desperate.

I don't mention to her what Jim said — about the jerk-off club. Andrea would say that it is too soon to worry about something like that.

"YOU'RE SO DESPERATE for affection, I think you'd love anyone who'd let you."

We were in the kitchen, cleaning up after supper. She washed, I dried the dishes. I remember the dishes. They were white porcelain, wedgewood, with a border of tiny green leaves, and in the center of each plate was a tiny bouquet of flowers, blue, yellow, pink. Her husband slept on the couch in the living room. I was sixteen, a virgin. If the word applies to men.

She spoke her words casually, as if they contained not one bit of malice towards me. She spoke as if she were merely making some mild observation about my appearance, the color of my shirt, the cut of my hair. I never forgot those words.

Every time I feel myself falling in love with someone, I'd remember that night, and wonder if maybe she wasn't right. No love affair has ever been completely free of the ghost of her words hovering between my lover and me.

I have never been the first person to say "I love you." I read once somewhere that the audacity of humility was to be the first person to say "I love you." But whenever I've wanted to say those words, I've thought of that night. I have always been afraid of being wrong, of not knowing what it means to love someone, how it was different from merely needing someone to hold you because you were lonely or feeling as if you hated yourself.

"You're so desperate, you'd love anybody," she said as she washed the dishes. I proved her right, and seduced her husband. He was a dreadful lover, selfish and incapable of affection. He was my first. It was an act of hate.

DANIEL AND I on my bed, my hands, resting against his thigh, the thigh I wanted to touch the night we met. He touches my arm, warm against my skin, his fingers, moving up to my shoulder, down to my wrist, his fingers encircle my wrist, trace the lines of my hand, my palm, he presses his mouth to my palm, kisses the tips of my fingers, glances into my eyes, then looks away.

Is he afraid, am I to—what?—be careful, your

eyes, don't stare at his eyes, remember, don't need too much, remember, you are not desperate.

"Would you like to stay tonight?" I ask.

Voice, his voice in my memory, Daniel, singing, the scene in the church, from *Tosca*, "You make me forget God," I remember his voice fills the room with its richness, Blue Lady, "How much room?" he is singing, I want to put my hands in the sound, to touch his chest, I remember, his legs, my fingers, moving over the keys, the piano, he sings, *"Mi fai dimenticare Iddio,"* I remember her words, "How much room?"

"Would you like to stay tonight?" I ask.

He kisses my face, my cheek, just above the line of my beard, I take his hands in mine, press them against my chest. I am not bad. I am not bad.

I touch his nipples, feel them harden beneath his shirt, he pulls me down on top of him, his hands, encircle my waist, rest on my hips, he presses his body into mine, holds his cock against mine.

He kisses my mouth, I feel the muscles of his legs, I press him against me, move beneath his body, he covers me over, covers me over, his hands, holding the back of my neck, my hands, touching his back, the black hair covering his back, my arms, pull him against me, closer. I lose the voices, lose myself, I cover me over, I lose myself in his body, he loses himself in me.

HE IS SLEEPING. What will Andrea say? Already I am

wondering if I did the right thing. It isn't a question of morality; if Andrea tells me I shouldn't have slept with him, it will be for other reasons. She may tell me that it is too soon. She may be afraid that I will feel too much too soon, and scare him.

But I am prepared to defend myself. I make Andrea a list, a list of all the things I didn't do:

I didn't tell him he was beautiful.

I didn't stare at him too much.

I didn't ask him "what it means," now that we have slept together.

I didn't ask him when I'll see him again.

I didn't risk my health.

Now I know what Jim meant the night of the audition, the night I met Daniel, about his being "AIDS paranoid." But Daniel isn't paranoid. We merely agreed to have safe sex; we didn't suck or fuck, and both of us came in the air. And afterwards, he washed my body.

"Be careful you don't put your hands near your mouth. Not until you've washed them," he said as he rinsed the soap from my cock. We stood together under the shower. I leaned up against him, resting my head on his shoulder. He washed me as carefully as if I were his child. He is so different; not like the men who get up to wash and leave you alone in bed, staring at the ceiling. He is so gentle.

But I try not to think about that too much. Don't be so intense, Andrea would say. Give him a chance to get to know you, and give yourself the same chance with him.

He sings beautifully. I loved playing the piano for him, hearing his voice so close to me. He sang from *Tosca,* Scarpia's aria in the church, "Tosca, you make me forget God." I thought of the Blue Lady. Love never makes me forget God. Only remember.

I wanted to ask him about the other thing Jim mentioned, about the jerk-off club. What could he possibly do at that club? Probably jerk-off with other guys. But it seems so unlike him, so unlike what I know of him. Looking at him sleeping, he seems so vulnerable, almost child-like. I wonder what he thinks of me.

Wait. The hardest thing to do in the world is to wait and do nothing. I kiss his sleeping face on the cheek, then close my eyes.

INFATUATION

I love you more than money,
and that's pretty noble
for a guy who chews toothpicks
and mends his pants with pins.

Our most intimate dialogues
are still in rehearsal.
They are games
my brain plays
at every subway delay.

"I love you" may sound
like a noisy campaign promise,
but my love is not a slogan.

And the spaces in me
are only river beds
waiting for this dry spell to pass,
not black space holes
sucking victims like air.

I love you
for the way you eat
a peach, for the
teasing songs
your body hums
beneath my nervous hands,
for the single green olive
that slips from your fingers
to plate, to lap,
to indifferent floor,
and rolls accusingly away.

I study the shapes
of your open hand
and notice five new worlds.

I am a collector
of casual gestures.
Your smiles make patterns
that spill like rain,
staining my mouth, my
eyes, my skin.
I am the keeper
of elusive gifts.
If this isn't love,
who cares?

Michael was snoring, lightly. As he slept, I studied
his face, the feathery, ash-colored lashes and

eyebrows, the broad nose, the pouting mouth. This is what it means, to love someone, I thought, to memorize his face while he sleeps, after you've made love.

I laid my head on his chest, and felt his lungs move up and down. One, two, three, I counted the breaths of his sleep, felt his breath against my face.

Every night with Michael I did these things, so that I would never forget what it felt like to be in love. I was so afraid of forgetting. So many years, seventeen, I had been all alone. And I knew that one day, I would be alone again. But then I would have my memories to save me.

From the very first night we met, I knew that Michael would be leaving me. That is why I took so much time, memorizing his face, his clothes, the cracked marble blue of his eyes. I pretended as if it weren't true, tried everything I could to prevent it. But I knew. He had to go back west, to school, to his other lover.

It doesn't make sense, knowing the man who will love you forever will also leave you. Or maybe it does, if you hate yourself, or think that you are bad.

I AM SITTING at the dining room table in Randy and Brian's apartment. Brian is reading the *Wall Street Journal*. Randy is in the kitchen, scrambling the eggs for breakfast.

The dining room table. Beneath its glass are photographs, in each one, two men smile out at the

camera. They are both in their early thirties—
Daniel's age. Handsome, tan, slim, their arms are
linked around each other. Randy and Brian near the
Colosseum. Randy and Brian on the beach in Nice.
Randy and Brian at a bar in Hawaii. I wonder if I
will ever have photographs like these, my arms linked
around someone, the both of us smiling.

Randy calls me into the kitchen. "Would you ask
Brian if he wants some coffee?"

I return to the dining room. Brian is reading
Barron's. Would you like some coffee? He nods his
head. I walk back into the kitchen.

"So, does he have a big one?"

I am telling Randy about my date with Daniel,
how well he sings, how he makes me laugh at rehearsals, saying his lines with different accents. "I do, I
luff you wery much." "Aye do, Aye luv you verrry
much."

"But was it a big one?"

Whenever I tell either Randy or Brian about a
man I am seeing, the first thing they ask is always
"How big was his dick?" or "Was it a big one?" or
"How many inches?" They know how I will respond
to the question. My answer is always the same.

"You know I don't care about that."

"Would you ask the one in the dining room if he
wants jam with his croissants?"

I walk back to the table. Brian is reading *The
Sunday Times.* Would you like some jam? He nods. I
walk back into the kitchen.

"I hope your new boy friend has at least got

money. As long as he's rich, I approve. Otherwise, once you get sick of each other, you're stuck with nothing to do. Look at Brian and me. I should've found somebody rich."

"You know you don't mean that."

He carries the food into the dining room, setting a plate on each of the three woven placemats. The irises in the glass pitcher are just beginning to open, they remind me of purple fingers curling in the air.

Brian looks up from his paper. "You know I hate raspberry jam."

What are they fighting about today? There is no point in asking. Neither one will answer me as long as the other is still in the room. Besides, it doesn't really matter. It is always the same fight:

Brian says Randy is selfish, inconsiderate. Randy says Brian doesn't want him anymore. Brian says he is tired, or sick, or depressed, or under too much pressure. Randy says Brian would be only too happy to trick with someone younger, hotter, better hung, new. If there were no such thing as AIDS.

Both of them are afraid of dying. Each one thinks the disease is already growing inside him, waiting. All those years of anonymous sex, the hundreds of men—it is only a matter of time. Bathrooms, bars, movie theatres, together, separately, in groups. They met at the baths five years ago, and have been together ever since. But monogamy has never been a part of their relationship. Sex is a sport, meant to be enjoyed. That is what being gay means—there are no rules. We are not our parents. Everyone has a right to determine how he will treat his own body. As long as no one gets hurt.

But that was before this terrible disease started killing off all their friends. They showed me a home movie once from a summer on Fire Island, a swimming pool, and men, tan, attractive, they are resting on rafts, splashing in the water. I recognize Randy, someone is tugging down the back of his suit, he flashes at Brian, filming the party.

Now, most of these men are dead. And together, Randy and Brian had slept with many of them.

"I hope you didn't tell Daniel you wanted to get married to him," says Randy.

No, I was well-behaved — no questions, no meaningful stares, no demands. And I don't even know his telephone number.

"Just take things slowly. Relax, enjoy the time you spend together. That way, you won't scare him off."

What is it inside me that scares other men? The years between Michael and now were filled with men who said I was too intense, men who said I wanted too much.

I am not bad. The Blue Lady tells me I am not bad, that my love is not poison. Someday I will meet someone who will not be afraid of what is inside me. But I must learn how to wait. That is part of what she means, when she asks me, "How much room?" She wonders if my heart is big enough to love someone slowly, expansively, in his own time. One day after another.

She asks so much. Sometimes her fingers feel sharp as knives. And even though I made her up, I wonder sometimes if I'm bleeding inside. But I am glad to know her. Every day, her hands teach me more. Every day, I learn how to live with the pain of her fingers measuring the room inside me, touching my heart.

"DON'T SAY I never gave you anything," said Michael as he handed me two silver discs from among the coins in his pocket. He was buying me an ice cream cone. The discs were washers, the metal kind used in building with wood. I put them on a chain around my neck, a chain I wore for the next few years.

Michael and I were in love with each other from the very first night we met. Or so I told myself later. Every night that summer he took me to bars. We drank gin and tonic, and danced, but only if he was drunk enough. Then he would wrap his arms around my waist, lift me off the floor, and spin me around the room. I thought it was so romantic.

"Pick up your feet when you walk."

He was the man I had been waiting for all of my life. He was the one who was going to save me, the one who would love me forever. I knew it from the moment we met.

"Your pants are too tight. Jesus, I'm embarrassed to be seen with you."

Michael believed that part of loving me meant changing me. I believed it too. I didn't care that he sometimes hurt my feelings, or made me feel like a freak.

"What the fuck are you so afraid of? Jesus Christ, grow up."

He followed me into the men's room. The light was white, that eerie fluorescence that makes your face look flat and dull. In front of the mirror, someone was combing his hair over and over again.

I stepped up to the urinal while Michael looked on. He stood near the door, with his arms folded across his chest. I unzipped my pants, and pulled myself free of the white cotton briefs I wore for him, because he said they made me look younger. Looking down, I saw myself dangling helplessly in the air. Oh God, if no one talks to me, I will be able to just go through with this and get out of here. I closed my eyes and concentrated. Finally I was able to go.

I hated using public restrooms, especially urinals, especially in gay bars. I was too shy to enjoy some other man staring at me as I peed. But Michael cured me of my shyness. He harrassed me until the shame I felt was worse than whatever might happen at a urinal.

"Please don't call me."

Often, we spoke of his other lover, his friend back west at art school. I knew everything about this man: the color of his hair, how he and Michael had met, what kind of music he liked. I even knew that he was uncircumcised. But he knew nothing about me. Not even that I existed. That was our agreement. In exchange for being loved by Michael, I was to remain a secret. I was to know everything while this other man knew nothing. And when Michael left to return to school, I was never to call or write him. We would speak only when Michael decided it was convenient for him.

"I love you."

In the years that Michael and I were lovers, I saw him only on his vacations from school. But I didn't mind it too much. The only thing that mattered to me was that he loved me. And I know he did. He told me so all the time. At least, at first.

That was the really terrible thing, the thing I could never understand. Michael said he loved me. But he also loved someone else. I would not have believed it was possible if I hadn't heard it myself, seen the tears, the anguish it caused him to be in love with two people at once, to know how much it hurt me.

The man who was supposed to save me was not supposed to love someone else. My father never loved another woman. Three infant sons, a sick wife, and through it all, he was faithful to her. Nothing I had ever known could possibly have prepared me for loving Michael.

But I knew I had no right to feel anything but lucky. I was lucky to be loved by him. I was lucky that he had the patience to love someone like me, someone who needed to be saved. I had no business feeling sorry for myself. And I knew from the very first night we met that Michael had another lover. I thought that somehow everything would work out, if we were really in love, if it was meant to be. I had no right to feel anything but gratitude. "Thank you for saving my life." That much I had learned from my parents; to be grateful for being loved.

That summer, when I was seventeen, the summer that I met Michael, that was the first time I spoke to her. I went into my parents' bedroom, and knelt before her statue. The statue was cracked at the base; it had fallen once from my mother's dresser. My father had tried to fill the crack with glue, but I could still make out a tiny fracture near the foot. I prayed that summer to the Blue Lady. I begged her to make things better. I told her I would do anything—drop out of high school, move west, even do something my parents would never have done, force myself to learn to love two people at once, Michael and his lover—just so that Michael might still love me. If Michael's love could not save me, maybe her love could.

But the Blue Lady never answered me. Or if she did, I couldn't hear whatever it was she said to me.

Eventually, Michael decided that loving two men was too difficult for him. And so, after two years of waiting by the telephone, two years of not one single letter, two years of touching no one else, two years of trying to let him save me, of changing my walk, the clothes I wore, the way I parted my hair, the way I went to the bathroom—I was alone again. I turned my back on the Blue Lady. We didn't speak again. Not for nine long years.

But I always knew Michael would leave me, even

though I prayed to her, even though I did everything possible to make him stay and love me. I knew he would leave me because I was bad. My love drove people away from me. That was why my mother went to the hospital for thirty-three days (as many as Christ had years): because I loved her too much.

Oh, Momma, I hug you and . . . That was why I had to be careful not to look too deeply into someone's eyes, or let him know I loved him. Maybe that was the real reason why I was never the first person to say those words, "I love you." My love was something to be feared.

But all of this is years ago, before Andrea, before Daniel, before I understood the Blue Lady's words. Before I knew about the pain. Now it is just a bad dream. Now I am waiting to learn what it means, to love someone and not be afraid, to love someone without being desperate.

SOMETIMES, when I am tired of the voices in my head, and Randy is busy, and my appointment with Andrea is five or six days away, I try writing poems. They are always conversations with myself, and almost always about men. I think of them as little stories, as variations of talking to myself, different ways of saying "I'm feeling lousy," or "You make me angry," or "Shut up and leave me alone," or "I'm falling in love with you." They are better than just talking; the words are different. Fewer, but more special. More careful. Maybe even safer. Like the story of the

Blue Lady's hands, my poems help me to remember important things.

Today, I write a little one about being saved. It has to be short, otherwise I'll say too much, and when I show it to Randy, he'll say, "Please. Cut out all that love shit. It sounds like a Hallmark card." He usually likes my poems, though I'm not always sure he knows what to make of them. Brian never understands them. But he always likes the ones about him, as long as Randy tells him first that he's in them. Otherwise, I don't think he would recognize himself.

I wrote one once about how Brian in the morning reminds me of Jesus. I see the sadness around his eyes, and the lines in his hands, and the way his mouth looks when he first wakes up, and I imagine how Jesus must have felt. All the love and sadness that he must have kept inside him all those years. And how his friends must have loved to feel his hands on them, to know their sadness and feel it, warm, against their faces.

In the poem, I imagine that I am in love with someone who reminds me of Jesus.

LOVE POEM

Mornings, he comes to me.
Wrapped in the
blue shadow rags
of dying night,
he offers
the gift of his hands,

the grey of his eyes,
the shapes
of muscles pushing up and out
like seeds beneath the earth.
Seeds too rich for earth,
the shapes of muscles.

Mornings, he is Jesus,
brushing the dark
from my forehead,
washing away
my sleep with spittle.
Mornings he feeds me
the gift of his hands.

Palm to palm we press
and mouths,
touching beneath the
blue shadow rags
of dying night,
our hands
tasting the shapes
of muscle and skin.
Palm I press
to mouth and nose,
drinking his hands,
breathing his skin.

Oh, the secrets we share
like sweet oranges,
promises traveling
from his mouth to mine.
He presses
his gentlest words
to my cheek,
or warms them against my throat.

Their liquid beauty
spreads through my skin,
washing away
all iniquity.

Even the bedclothes
recognize the
grace of his feet
in the mornings,
and the kindness
of his face
is never wasted.

Mornings, he comes to me.
Wrapped in the
blue shadow rags
of dying night,
he offers his hands
like a gift of water.
Mornings, he is Jesus,
feeding me
the gift of his hands.

Randy always teases me about that poem.

"Why don't you write one about me? Oh, I know, because I'm not Brian. You like Brian better than me. You think Brian is Jesus Christ."

Here is today's poem. I write it because as much as I don't need to be saved anymore, there is that small part of me that gets tired sometimes.

Dear Mom and Dad . . .

"Thank you for saving my life
so many times," she wrote him
one birthday. He tells me
I am my mother's son,
and I wonder when
they'll take me to Bellevue
for asking some
smart ass
slim-hipped, broad-backed
bossy kind of
guy
to save me
just a little.

"WHO TOLD YOU you're just like your mother?"

Oh, everyone. My grandpa. He thought so.
Though that isn't exactly what he said.

"You should've been born a girl." I was playing in
the kitchen, sitting on the floor. One of my hands
stirred the invisible cake batter with a wooden spoon.
The other held the mixing bowl. "You should've been
born a girl." I hated him for saying that. It made me
feel like some kind of freak.

And my father used to say it all the time. Whenever I felt sad or lonely, he would say, "You're just
like your mother." He never understood how it felt,
to want other people to like you. He never cared
what anyone else thought or said about him. He liked
himself just the way he was. And he thought everyone

else was just like him. Except my mother and me.

I remember once hearing the family doctor tell my mother I was most like her. He divided up the whole family into two groups; those who resembled my father, and those who resembled her. I was the only one in her group. Both my brothers were more like my father than I was.

And I told it to myself, too. I wanted to be like her. I loved to sit with her and fold the laundry. And whenever she washed the dishes, she sang so well. She liked hearing me play the piano. Not like my brothers. She never asked me to play softer, so she could hear the television. Why shouldn't I have wanted to be like her? And maybe I needed to feel like her. Maybe I knew even then that I was different from my father and brothers. Maybe I needed some way to explain to myself the fact that I was gay.

"Do you still believe you're gay because of her?"

No, of course not. I don't have any idea why I love men. I imagine it has to do with a combination of many things. But I have never wanted to be straight. I always thought it was a good thing, that I loved men. They seem to need to be loved so much more than women. Besides, I never thought that I was all that different from my parents. Except that I am gay.

"What about your mother? Did she tell you you were just like her?"

No. My mother hated herself. She would never have wanted her children to be anything like her. It's a shame. There was so much to love about her.

"Why did she tell you about her breakdown?"

She always said it was so that we wouldn't be afraid, so that if we ever needed to talk to someone about something that was troubling us, we wouldn't feel scared or ashamed. She wanted to spare us some of the pain she had felt, the years of being too shy to speak about the things that bothered her. And I guess she needed someone to talk to about it. My father was away at work. My brothers were too young, or not really interested. I was anxious to listen. I was glad that she confided in me. It made me feel closer to her.

"How are things going with Daniel?"

Fine. We've seen each other every weekend for the past few weeks, plus at rehearsals. I think the play is going to be cancelled. The dialogue is terrible, and no one wants to put up any money for it. I hope it isn't, though. I like knowing I will see him at least once a week.

I enjoy the time I spend with him very much. But I never ask any questions. I try and just take it one day at a time.

"Good. It sounds like you're doing just fine. Keep it up."

Andrea gets up from her chair. That is the signal that my hour is over. I reach in my pocket and pull out thirty dollars.

"Thanks. I'll see you next week."

WE HEAR at the next rehearsal that the play is being

"postponed." We will not be rehearsing for awhile. At first, I am frightened. Will he still want to see me? I try to calm my fear with what I have learned from Andrea.

> You can't trick someone into caring about you. If he doesn't want to see you now that the show is off, then he probably didn't want you to begin with. There are other men. You are not desperate.

Daniel asks if he is still welcome at my house for Saturday. Of course, I say. I am ashamed of myself for being so insecure, for thinking so little of our friendship. Where have I learned to be so mistrustful of other people's affection for me?

For two months now, we have seen each other almost every weekend. He comes over Saturday and sings all day, and usually stays the night. And I have been so good. I still don't even know his telephone number. The most I will allow myself to say is that I enjoy the time we spend together. He nods, and smiles.

In some ways, he is a difficult man to get to know. He asks no questions about my past, and volunteers nothing about his own.

"Tell me about your childhood. Tell me about your family."

"What do you want to know?"

He is not put off by my questions; but he never speaks about these things unless I ask him first. I wonder if he hasn't been hurt by someone, hurt so deeply that he is reluctant to talk.

The only times I have seen him really relaxed are when he is singing, or when he is in bed with me. When he sings, the richness of his voice fills the room. His eyes are so bright and clear, and his whole body seems to be opening up like a flower. Then he allows himself to feel the wonder of his own sound. I try not to watch him too closely while he sings. I don't want to make him self-conscious; and I am afraid of feeling too much too soon. He seems so vulnerable, almost childlike, when he sings.

And in bed, he is so tender. Having "safe sex" prevents us from doing many of the usual things, and so we spend hours just touching each other's bodies. He kisses my hands and feet, plays with the hairs at the back of my neck, presses his cock against my belly. I know he wants to be inside me. I know I would let him, if there were no such thing as AIDS. It is exciting, knowing he denies himself this pleasure for my sake, so I will stay healthy. If he asked to fuck me, I would probably let him. We could use rubbers; I'm sure we will, eventually. I want to feel him inside me.

SUNDAY MORNING, we are lying in bed. We have just made love, washed ourselves off, and gotten back under the covers. He rolls on his side, facing me.

"I belong to a jerk-off club. We meet every week, though I haven't been going since we started rehearsals. It's totally safe, and lots of fun. What do you think of that?"

Oh my God, Jim was right, this is the moment I have dreaded for weeks. Don't say anything. Don't speak until you are absolutely certain of what you should say. You will destroy everything you've worked for all these weeks if you overreact. Think of how much time it has taken him to feel as if he could trust you with this. So what if he belongs to this club? He hasn't been going since you started dating. It is totally safe, and it is better for him than sleeping with strangers. How much room? Remember, remember her fingers. Remember why you tell the story of the Blue Lady's hands. Her fingers have knocked the wind out of me this time. You don't know why he goes. Remember, he's Randy and Brian's age. You are not your parents. Everyone has a right. No one is getting hurt. Damn her. It is too soon. If you say too much, you will regret it. It is too soon, to make demands.

"That sounds interesting," I smile. "I had heard you belonged to a club." I kiss him lightly on the cheek.

So what if Jim was right? The Daniel I know is not "dirty" or irresponsible or shallow. He is gentle and funny and kind. So what if he belongs to this club? Guys his age think differently than you do about sex. Remember Randy's words, sex is a sport, meant to be enjoyed. Monogamy is the invention of repressed Catholics who hate homosexuals like us. You have no right to make demands. Not just yet; it is too soon.

And he said he doesn't go anymore. Not since you started dating.

I AM SITTING on the couch at Randy and Brian's apartment. Their VCR is recording "Wall Street Week" for Brian, who is still at his office. Randy is watering the plants.

"I'm telling you, he doesn't want me anymore."

Randy and Brian are fighting again. It has been months since they've made love. Brian says he's depressed about AIDS. Another of their friends has died.

> "I saw him just three weeks ago. Then tonight his lover called me to tell me he'd died. Pneumonia," Brian said. Brian and I were sitting on the couch. Randy was away, visiting his parents in Miami. Brian stared ahead of himself and said nothing for awhile. I wanted to tell him that it would be all right. I wanted to tell him that I loved him. But I was afraid of how he would react. He is so stoic. I think we are both afraid of his emotions. Only Randy sees him cry. "I'll stay on the couch tonight, if you like," I said.

"I know he's upset about Thomas dying. But it's been almost two months now. And this started even before he died." Randy waters the African violets.

Brian needs a therapist. Randy and I have agreed on this fact for almost a year now. He doesn't know how to show his feelings. He can't express affection for the people he loves. And I don't doubt for a moment that he loves Randy.

"It's his father. If you met his father, you'd know why he is the way he is."

But I have my own ideas. For years, Brian has behaved as if sex were something "dirty," something that happened between strangers, in bathrooms or dark back-rooms, a sport where the players were nameless asses, faces, cocks, tits. All those years of treating sex as if it were something to be done in secret. All those years of needing to touch and hold another man, and thinking that this was the only way.

No wonder he doesn't want to sleep with Randy. Brian loves Randy. If sex is something you do with strangers, then you don't fuck the man you love. If sex is something disgusting, something that happens in toilets or bars, then you don't have sex with your lover. Love and affection you get from him. Sex you get somewhere else. Sex isn't love; Brian knows that.

But I don't say any of this to either Randy or Brian. Randy would tell me I am repressed, judgmental, afraid of my own sexuality—all the things he learned back in the seventies, in his bisexual rap group. Brian would say it is "natural" for men to want numerous sex partners; only women prevent straight men from acting just like us. "You're not your parents," they would say. "I'm not you," I would say.

"How is Daniel?" Randy asks.

Fine. We see each other once a week. I still don't

know his telephone number.

I don't tell Randy about the club, about how it bothers me. It is too soon. And I'm not in the mood for a lecture on how uptight I am.

"It sounds like things are going well," he says. "Aren't you glad you didn't tell him you wanted to get married? Just relax. Enjoy yourself."

This is the poem I write for Brian, because I was afraid, because I didn't know how to tell him how sorry I was that his friend Thomas died.

DEATH IN AUTUMN

Magic, this spectacle
death of leaves.
They swallow the sun fire
summer months,
autumn turn transparent
spill out their burning blood
before our eyes
a red death show
sienna brown grey
the ashes, ashes
covering the ground.

Not like us.
Not like the lovers we lost,
stolen away in the night
while the gaping moon looked on,
fish-eyed moon
holding her hollow womb, screaming
her silent white song.

Matthew, whose lungs collapsed
in a poisonous sleep,
Joseph, who slipped and disappeared,
and James, who cut himself open
to kill his disease of bruises.

All of them gone,
leaving no letters
etched in those desperate hours
when names of God
rattle the empty air
as if He might appear, gone,
not in flames, but softly,
no feast of blood,
no scream of colors,
but taken from us
like the many dreams
we can't recall upon waking.

What thief God
would make so small a thing
of a young man's death,
and who will we lose
when we next look away,
forgetting that final goodbye,
that meeting of arms,
sweet performance of mouths,
words we horde for winter,
love we waste, love
we hide in our hands?

HE TURNS THE KEY in the lock, and pushes the door
open. Before he steps inside the room, he removes
his shoes. I do the same.

It is a small apartment—bedroom, kitchen, living room, bath. Fresh patches of white plaster are smeared over the beige walls waiting to be repainted. Some of the furniture is covered with plastic throws, and the lamps in the living room are still wrapped in brown paper, the paper in which they were purchased. The wooden floors are in the process of being refinished. The old varnish has been removed; now the stain must be stripped.

There are piles of magazines and books scattered around the apartment, and plastic bags filled with things—pictures, old clothing, and some strange-looking metal and plastic things, tools of some sort, I guess.

"I'm sorry about the apartment. But with rehearsals and everything, I haven't been able to finish decorating."

"It's nice," I say.

This is the first time Daniel and I have stayed at his place. I congratulate myself. He is so protective of his privacy; it is obvious from the unfinished state of his place that very few people ever see the inside. I am glad he has asked me home with him.

Beneath all the throws, the furniture looks to be almost new—brass, black lacquer, and glass. And all around the apartment are small things, objects he has arranged here and there to make him feel at home while he finishes decorating: photographs propped up on the kitchen counter, Daniel dressed in a tuxedo, sea shells piled up near the bathtub, on the commode. And a print, Van Gogh's bedroom at

Arles, hanging on the bedroom wall. I stare at all these things whenever he isn't looking, try to learn what I can from them about his life.

'Do you like this color?" he asks, indicating his blue shower curtain. "I think it gives the room a nice touch. Kind of tranquil."

"It's nice," I say.

"I'm really sorry about the mess. Maybe we should've stayed at your place?"

He is probably seeing his home through my eyes, wondering how it became so disordered. But that is not what I'm seeing at all. He is so adorable, asking me how I like the shower curtain.

"Would you like something to drink?"

He is nervous. He looks at me almost as if to say, "What are you doing here?" as if he's forgotten who I am and why he's invited me to stay the night. I must do something to make him relax, before he gets too uncomfortable.

"I like to take my clothes off when I'm home," he says. "It makes me feel more comfortable. And it's better for the body, not to be too confined." He is unbuttoning his shirt.

"Here, let me help you," I say as I unbuckle his pants, and slip my hands down the front of his shorts.

WE ARE LYING IN BED. The headboard is covered with memories, a ceramic ashtray he built as a child, his hands, I see the marks of his eight-year-old hands in the clay. And cards, a birthday card from his parents; he is already a year old. He rubs the hair on my legs, begins to yawn, covers his mouth.

I prop myself up on my elbows. "What is all this?" I ask, gesturing towards one of the plastic bags, the bag filled with the strange metal and plastic gadgets.

"Didn't I tell you? I used to be a dentist."

"You're kidding me, right?"

"No. For about five years. I gave it all up to go into acting. The bags are filled with old equipment. I haven't had the chance to throw it away yet."

Should I be surprised? No, it makes sense. It makes sense that he would give up a "serious" profession to do what he wanted to do. He is that kind of man. And it makes sense that I would know him for months—well, two—before he remembered to tell me.

WE ARE LOOKING through his photograph album. Mostly, vacation pictures: Daniel on the beach in Puerto Rico, Daniel in the mountains of Nevada. But there is one of a boy of about sixteen or so. It is him, Daniel, as a teenager.

He smiles straight into the camera. He wears a crew neck sweater, and an oxford shirt. The same clear eyes, the same black hair, the mouth that makes me remember. The photo reminds me of being young. I remember the terrible crush I had on a dark boy back in the seventh grade. What is this strange feeling? You're not supposed to want other guys, want them in this unnamable way. I feel funny things, fingers, hands on my chest, what does it mean?

"It's you," I say.

"Yeah. But with more hair."

"No, it's you *now.*"

I see in the photograph the same thing I've seen in his face many times, whenever I have glanced at him sleeping, whenever he is on top of me, looking into my eyes for a moment. He is still that same boy.

Who has hurt you, Daniel? Who has made you so cautious, made you so reluctant to share yourself with me? I see it in the photograph, I see it in your eyes. I know you want to need me. Sometimes, when we are in bed together, you are almost like a child. You fall asleep holding my hand. And then mornings, you wake up touching my face.

"Sure, I've been hurt. But it's different for me. I'm older than you. I need more time."

Older. Too old to love someone? What do you want from me?

"But I'm pretty strong," he says.

"I wish sometimes you wouldn't be so strong. Not with me."

"I know."

"THE OVERWHELMING OTHERNESS OF WOMEN."

I read that today in an ad for a gay film. I wonder what it means. I have always found men to be somewhat of an "other" for me. Not physically, but certainly emotionally. I used to think that it was just straight men. But more and more I find that most men seem different from me. It isn't merely that they seem to want different things from sex than I do. It is something else, something deeper.

I didn't really know any boys, aside from my brothers, until I was eleven or so. I had male cousins and neighbors and schoolmates, but they were never really my friends. My closest friends were always girls. We played jump rope together at recess, we did our homework together, we ate together in the school cafeteria. Sometimes, I would go to their houses after school, or they would come to mine. I taught my friends to play songs on the piano, and they taught me how to knit with two paint brushes and a shoe lace. They never made me feel self-conscious about being a boy. At least not for a few years.

I hated it in school, when they divided up the class into two separate groups, girls and boys. I always wanted to be with the girls. The boys were stupid; they got bad grades, and they were always yelling and pushing each other. And they laughed at me, because I played with girls. I hated being laughed at, but whenever I complained to my parents, they would say "Do you like the way you are?" and I would say yes, I guess so, and they would tell me to ignore the teasing, and it would go away. But it didn't go away; it only got worse, with each passing year.

I could have probably taken all the teasing and

name calling, if my girl friends hadn't turned against me. In the fourth grade, things started to change. The girls would huddle together and talk about girl things, training bras and getting their periods and which boys they liked. And when I would try and listen in, they would push me away and tell me to go somewhere else. I got sick that year for about a week, and when I came back, they sneered at me.

"Look who's here. Too bad you got better."

At home, I was crying all the time. My parents were so concerned, they took me to the school social worker. He had a flat-top haircut, and horn-rimmed glasses like my father's, and I really wanted to tell him what was wrong. But every time I had an appointment, the principal stood nearby, listening. He was fat with ruddy skin and sour breath, and I decided I wasn't going to say anything in front of him. So when they asked me what was wrong, I just shook my head and said, "Nothing."

Finally, I decided that I couldn't stand it any longer; I had to find a friend who was a boy. So I picked one out one day from my class. He was new, and he didn't know that I used to play with girls. I didn't think he was very smart or fun to play with, but I was so desperate, I couldn't afford to be choosey. So we hung around together at recess, and occasionally we would go to each other's houses. Sometimes people would whisper about me and say,

"Didn't he used to play with girls?"

If anyone ever confronted me about it, I usually lied and said no, I never played with girls. Sometimes

I would see my old girl friends, and wonder what it was that I had done to make them hate me. But I never talked to them about it.

I had my first real male friend when I was twelve. But by that time, it was too late; I knew that the way I liked him was not the way boys usually like each other. He was handsome and smart and funny, and I knew he really liked me, even if it wasn't in the same way that I liked him. We remained friends for years. And eventually, I told him that I was gay. He was a little surprised, but he never made me feel weird or uncomfortable about it.

It is difficult to describe how I felt all those years. I didn't feel like a girl, but I didn't feel like other boys, either. I knew something was different about me. Once, I even asked my parents for a toy truck. I didn't really want it, but I hoped it would make them feel better about me, reassure them that I wasn't so different after all. It was even kind of fun, pretending to play with the truck. But it just wasn't the same as playing school, or pretending to cook.

Lots of gay men say they knew they were different from other boys at an early age. But my feelings of being different didn't go away, once I realized that there were other men like me, gay men. I still feel like an outsider, like a man who is and is not like other men. I talk about men sometimes as if I weren't one of them, as if their behavior is a mystery to me. And lots of times, I prefer the company of women to men. When I am with them, I am so much more comfortable with myself. I don't have to worry if I am attractive enough, or interesting enough, or masculine enough to be loved. They trust me, and I trust them. They aren't afraid to tell me what they need. And they listen to me. Andrea is a good example. I can't imagine telling another man the things I have told her.

I AM LYING in Daniel's lap, looking up into his face. His fingers travel over my mouth, around my nose, he traces my eyebrows, touches my lashes.

We have been singing most of the day, again, from *Tosca*. In the church, "You make me forget God." I think he would make a wonderful Scarpia, dark, handsome, mysterious. Now he is tired. We sit on the sofa, resting.

He gazes into my eyes, then looks away. His fingers touch the bridge of my nose, he brushes the hair from my forehead, presses his palm against my cheek, rubs the stubble of my beard.

I look into his eyes, then look away. My fingers touch his lower lip. He kisses my fingertips. I move my hand to his ears, pull the lobes gently, touch his hair, trace the grey at his temples.

He looks at me. His eyes fill with tears. Silently, they fall from his lashes, down his cheeks.

"What's wrong?"

"Nothing. I was looking at your face, and . . ."

I wipe his tears with my hands. I want him to tell me more, tell me how he feels, what he is thinking.

"I guess you got to me. I mean, I was looking at your face, and . . ." He laughs a small laugh. "That's all I want to say right now."

I say nothing. The Blue Lady tells me to keep my mouth shut. I rise up out of his lap, kiss his forehead, press his face against my chest. I take his hand in mine, and lead him off the sofa, into my bedroom.

He kisses my mouth. This is the hardest part of safe sex, the fact that we never kiss with our tongues. I want to taste his mouth, and I want to feel his tongue in my mouth. But he is afraid it may not be safe. I would be willing to take this risk now, tonight.

We fall down to the bed, pull away each other's clothes, throw them all over the floor. He is on top of me, pressing his cock against mine, kissing my neck. He speaks softly, I feel his warm breath against my ear.

"Is it okay if I fuck you? I'll wear a rubber, and I won't come inside you."

How many men have asked me if it's okay? Almost none. Usually, they just assume I'm willing to do whatever they'd like.

"I'd like that. I'd like that a lot."

He slips the rubber over his cock. He enters me, slowly. There is almost no pain. I relax, I want him this way, inside me.

As he moves into me, I watch his mouth, remember God in His generous moods, I touch his back, feel the hair on his back, feel his sweat, I remember the first time, how I touched his back.

"How much room?" asked the Blue Lady. I open

up, and take him inside me.

I HAVE NEVER been the first person to say "I love you."
I have always been too afraid. But this time, I want
to be the one. If Daniel and I should fall in love, I
will be the one to say it first. I make that promise to
myself.

"I LOVE YOU."

Michael and I were lying in bed. He was leaving
in just a few days. For the very last time, he was
going back west, back to his other lover.

"I love you," I said.

The man who would love me forever was leaving
the way I knew he would, which doesn't make sense
unless you hate yourself, unless you think you are
bad, unless you believe your love is poison. But that
was before, and now, just a bad dream.

"I love you," I said.

It was not like my parents. It was never like my
parents. He never left her. Three infant sons, and

"I love you," I said.

Now I would have only memories to save me, I
memorized his face while he slept, I

"I love you," I said.

"You're only saying that to annoy me," he
answered.

Andrea says I could tell a hundred men that I
loved them, and I probably still would never hear

someone say those words again. But that's what I fear. Sometimes, when I say those words in my head, I hear his voice in response. Those words, "I love you," seem almost incomplete without his response. "You're only saying that to annoy me."

I know it wasn't his fault. I know he felt guilty about leaving me, and he didn't want to be reminded of it. But I was so young. And he was the first man I'd ever really loved.

I could make a list of all the stupid things people have said to me, stupid, heartless things that echoed in my mind for years. But those echoes are almost gone now. There will be no list. I am too old to continue this running battle with Michael, with her and her "You're so desperate," with all the old voices hovering around inside my head.

WE ARE SITTING at the breakfast table in my kitchen. Daniel is teasing me. He takes a bite out of his croissant, then grabs his mouth as if he has lost a tooth.

"Are they too hard?" I ask. "I guess I overcooked them."

He grabs my hand across the table, squeezes it for a moment, then lets it go. I am so happy this morning. Little by little, we are growing closer. I have learned to wait. And I will not forget last night, his tears, how gently he entered me.

"I have something to show you," I say.

I open up an old notebook to a page marked with a slip of paper. The handwriting is my own. It is one of my journals, from about six years ago. After Michael. Before Daniel. I show him the page, and read it aloud.

WANTED

one male, age 20–30
not fat, not ugly
intelligent, talented, artistic
honest, sensitive, gentle, vulnerable
possessing an innocence toward life
hard working, resourceful, thoughtful
possessing a sense of humor and a sense
of optimism.
serious, strong, resilient, creative
comfortable with silence
not afraid to be wrong or make mistakes
able to make commitments
responsible. full of character
viewing life with a seemingly naïve eagerness
that is actually an eternal hopefulness
kind, considerate, a bit awkward
with beautiful eyes
unafraid to take risks
with a deep and profound commitment to
sharing himself with another person
and anxious to take all that I have
to share with him.

Is this asking the impossible? *NO.*

"I WROTE that when I was twenty. Some of it sounds like a description of you."

What would Andrea say? Is this too much too

soon? I like him. I want him to know that.

"Gee, you're right, it does sound like me. And Superman. Except that I am over thirty." He laughs, brushes a stray hair out of my eyes. He reaches into his pocket.

"Now that you've shown me something of yours, let me show you something of mine."

I read the first sentence, and feel the Blue Lady's fingers piercing my skin.

The Club Newsletter for November
Box 6961
New York, NY 10025
November 1, 1988

CELEBRATE OUR SECOND ANNIVERSARY
THE SHOT HEARD AROUND THE WORLD

MEMBERS ONLY
Saturday, November 12th, 9:30 PM to Midnight

Cum to *The Club's* Annual Anniversary Party. Check in is at 9:00. Doors will close by 9:45. There'll be plenty of food, plenty of lube, and plenty of hot men, so be sure to attend.

CELEBRATE THE INTERNATIONAL
EJACULATION EMANCIPATION
RUB DICK WITH ALL YOUR J.O. BUDDIES
THIS SATURDAY NIGHT

OTHER NEWS

1. Attendance at our weekly meetings is tripling. Be sure your guests follow the rules—no heads

below the belt, no drugs, no fisting or fucking.

2.   Members are allowed only one guest; please
     don't bring someone you don't know. We love
     new members, but only if they're ready to strip
     and get into the group action.

3.   *The Club's* own artist, *Hans Pieter,* is audition-
     ing buddies for his new j.o. film. Contact him if
     you're interested in pounding your meat on the
     wide silver screen.

HAPPY ANNIVERSARY TO ALL OUR MEMBERS
SEE YOU SATURDAY NIGHT AT 9:30

He handed me the newsletter as if it were some
kind of greeting card. Jesus, how can he be so innocent.

"I'm going to the party on Saturday night. It
should be fun."

The Blue Lady's fingers are wicked this morning, like knives, too tight, I want to pull myself free
of her hands.

"What's the matter?" he asks.

"Nothing."

"Of course something's the matter. I can see it in
your face. Did we have plans for Saturday night?"

Did we have plans for Saturday night? He
doesn't even realize how this feels. Her hands twist
around inside me, make me feel like puking, make
me feel as if I can't breath. I am so afraid.

Be careful. In just a few minutes you could destroy everything you have with him, everything you've
worked for, the weeks of waiting, never learning his
phone number, never asking "what it means," now

that you are sleeping together. What do I say? Take your time. Remember. Remember everything you have learned.

"I'm sorry that I can't present my best self to you about this. It's just so foreign to me."

Good. The words sound like something your psychiatrist taught you to say, but at least you were honest.

"But you knew I belonged to this club. I joined before we even met. You never said it bothered you."

"That's because I never knew *when* you were going."

All those nights we weren't together, all the nights there were no rehearsals, I may have suspected that he was there. But I never knew it for a fact. Now I had to look forward to Saturday night, to feel the Blue Lady's claws poking around inside me, to imagine the party, imagine him touching other men, imagine them touching him, men who were taller, slimmer, more handsome, more intelligent, better hung, better built, better lovers than me.

He leads me by the hand, over to the sofa.

"It's just fun. I mean, it has nothing to do with us. I'm not exactly driven to go, but I'd like to be at this party. It's hot. It's kind of fraternal. Lots of my friends go. But it doesn't take the place of what we have."

"What do we have? We never talk about what we have."

Now I've done it. Oh God, I can see by the look on his face that he senses my panic and fear. I am not desperate. I am not desperate. I shouldn't have asked. I will not lose control.

"I don't think we should have to put words on what we have."

Typical frightened male response, afraid of being trapped, afraid of being tied down, afraid of being swallowed up by me. Back off, slow down, relax.

"You're right, you're absolutely right, it's much too soon in our—friendship." Calm down, I tell myself. "But I need to know that you enjoy the time you spend with me."

"Of course I enjoy the time I spend with you. Can't you tell by the way I act when we're together?"

"But you don't *tell* me."

"I don't think I should *have* to tell you."

This is going too far too fast, if I am not careful, Oh God, I must say something, lie, anything, something to give me more time, something to reassure him.

"I want you to go to the party. I would never ask you not to go. I am not that kind of person. I want you to go, and to have a good time. It's just that I need a little time to get used to the idea. You know, deep down, I'm too middle class. Randy says it all the time. I just need to get used to it."

My HEAD IS RESTING in his lap. He is stroking my forehead.

"I better go."

Oh, God, please tell me I didn't blow it, Blue Lady, forgive me, I am not bad, sometimes your fingers are too much for me.

"I'll call you later," he says. I walk him to the door. He kisses me on the mouth.

"I had a nice time last night. I enjoyed the time we spent together," he says.

Thank you, Blue Lady.

"Thanks. I had a nice time, too. I'll talk to you soon."

I close the door behind him.

HE GAVE you what you needed. That is the first thing Andrea will say. You told him you needed to be reassured, and he reassured you. Of course he cares for you. Pay attention to how he treats you.

What the hell am I going to do? A jerk-off club. Every time I envision him touching another man, I am furious. He lied to me. He made me believe he was vulnerable, child-like, innocent. How could he be all those things, and still go to that club?

How is what he does with those men different from what we have? All our "safe sex" — no fucking, no sucking — why is what we have different?

Does he cry in front of the members of his club? Andrea would ask. Does he spend the day with them singing, does he fall asleep holding their hands? Of course what the two of us have is incomparable to what goes on at that club.

I can leave him, because of this. I have the right

to leave him if I decide I can't handle this. It amounts to infidelity. Everyone has the right to determine what role sex will play in his life. Even me. I can demand monogamy.

But you have no agreement with him. You have no right to feel offended. Monogamy, fidelity—you never asked for either one. He has not betrayed you.

You are not your parents. Maybe your mother was a virgin when she married your father. But you are not them. You are too old to continue pretending, pretending that you have been in love with every man with whom you've had sex.

I am so afraid of losing him to this club. Almost afraid enough to leave him.

The boy in the photograph, the teenager, the dark boy with the clear eyes, the hair, the mouth that makes me remember. Is that Daniel? Or is he someone else, the men having sex in bathrooms and bars, the men who hate themselves, the men who behave as if they are ashamed, the dark places, the strangers.

"How much room?" the Blue Lady asks. Is your heart big enough? Maybe not. Maybe it is already too full. Maybe there is no more room. Can my heart be so small? I don't know. God, I don't know. I am not perfect, I am not a saint. Her fingers hurt like knives, it is like a sword inside me.

I hate being gay. I hate not fitting in, feeling separate, feeling like a freak. I am not anyone. I can't let someone save me. But I can't fuck in bathrooms, suck some stranger's cock through a hole in the wall.

Wait. I must wait. Blue Lady, please help me wait.

"SO, HOW ARE THINGS GOING?" she asks.

There is so much to talk about this week. But I know I will leave her office feeling better. No matter how bad I may feel at the beginning of the hour, by the time my appointment is over, I know I will feel better.

I tell Andrea everything, about the jerk-off club, how it frightens me, how I don't understand it, how I have the right to end my relationship with him, if I choose.

"Do you want to stop seeing him?"

No. My heart is not that small. I will not let my heart be that small. He is a wonderful man, sensitive, gentle, funny. I will not let myself destroy our friendship. I want to be closer to him.

"Does his going to the club take him away from you?"

No. He told me he would not allow it to interfere with us. He only goes occasionally. He says he could give it up. But he enjoys it, and I will not be the kind of person to tell him not to go. I want him to feel glad to be with me. I don't want to change him; not to suit me.

"So, what do you want?"

I want to understand it. I want it not to hurt so much. I want her fingers to ease up a little, not to pinch so sharply.

"You say his going to the club hurts you. How does it hurt you?"

I admit, I'm insecure. How can I possibly compete for his affection, with a room full of naked men?

"And I suppose you think they're all better than you, in some way."

So, it's not rational. So it's not likely that ALL of them are smarter, more attractive, more interesting than me. But some of them are bound to be. Maybe even most of them.

"You said that he's been going to this club since before the two of you met?"

Yes. For about a year and a half now, he's been going.

"If all those men are so much better than you, why isn't he dating them? He knew them before he met you."

"If you tell him to stop going because you're insecure, then you act on your insecurity. That means it's bound to get worse. You need for him to continue going to that club. You need to know, to find out, that even with the choice of all those other men, he still chooses to spend time with you. And if he doesn't choose you, then you need to know that, too."

But I'm not just afraid of losing him to another man in the club. I'm afraid of losing him to the whole thing.

"The whole thing?"

Back-room bars, baths, anonymous sex, sex in

bathrooms.

"If he really wanted those things, he'd be pursuing them. Do you think that somehow you're tricking him into spending time with you? He wants to get to know *you*. Not someone else."

But I know that before AIDS, he was just like Randy and Brian. Provincetown, Fire Island, Bloomingdale's, Grand Central Station. But he tells me he's reformed. He says that was empty, that he isn't interested in casual sex anymore.

"Look, if at one time he made a habit of sleeping with strangers, then the jerk-off club is a tremendous step for him. He knows the men in his club. He knows their names, their faces. He talks to them. The men in the club treat each other like people. Not just cocks and asses.

"It's tough, to be a gay man his age. The world was so different when he grew up. It was tougher then, to be gay. Homo*sexual*. That is what this society taught him: that he was sexual before he was anything else. So how do homo*sexuals* find the love and affection they need? They look for it in sex. And because society tells them they're sick, they look for it in dark places, in bathrooms, in back-room bars.

"You should be grateful, that the club exists for men like Daniel. Think of all the months before the two of you met. He had a place where he could feel good about himself, where he could express his sexual needs in a way that wasn't damaging to him."

Daniel alone, I imagine him, the face of the boy. Maybe he thought he was bad, maybe he hated himself for being alone. Daniel, I would press you into me, hold you inside my chest, to take away this pain. I would surround you, feel you moving inside me. And you would have nothing to be ashamed of.

"He's trying to change. He's doing everything he can. He told you he doesn't have sex with strangers anymore; he goes to his club. And he's dating you. Do you have enough patience to wait for him?"

The Blue Lady's fingers. Why did I make up her story? Can I bear her fingers inside me, can my heart.

"And maybe he gets off on the exhibitionist part of the club. Some guys are like that. It doesn't hurt anybody. And he can't really help it. People can't control what turns them on."

I dated someone once who used to expose himself in the park. Not to children, or anything like that. Just to other men who wanted to see. I didn't see the harm in that.

"Besides, it's almost funny, when you think of it. A group of grown men pulling on each other's cocks. Picture it in your mind. Doesn't it strike you as funny?"

She is right. There is something very funny about the whole thing. How does this woman know so much about how it feels, to be a gay man?

I AM THINKING about what Andrea said, I am trying to work this thing out. I know she is right about many things. But that doesn't change the pain in my chest, whenever I think about the club.

"What is it like?" I ask Daniel. Whenever we talk about it, I feel better. There is something about the way he speaks to me. It doesn't seem so scary or ugly whenever he describes it.

I know they check their clothes at the door. I know that the "safe sex" rules are strictly enforced. There is no kissing, or sucking or fucking, even with rubbers. Sometimes they jerk-off in pairs; sometimes in a group.

"It's not like a bar. The men are friendly. No one is forced to do anything he doesn't want. You can just watch, if you like. It's very fraternal."

I have so many other questions, questions I'm afraid to ask, about Daniel, about who he chooses to jerk-off with, does he touch them, does he let them touch him, is it anything like sex with me. But I can't ask those questions. Not yet. I need more time, to get used to the idea, to think about all the things Andrea said.

A BOY AND GIRL are walking down the street, hand in hand. He has dark hair and eyes, and wire-rimmed glasses. He wears blue jeans, and a high school varsity letter jacket. Her blue eyes are clear as water, and her brown hair sits on the top of her head in a high pony-tail. She wears jeans and a leather jacket, a jacket that looks as if it belongs to him. They are walking a dog, a beautiful Gordon Setter.

I am tired, feeling a little depressed. I am

jealous of them. I bet he doesn't belong to any jerk-off club. I bet she doesn't have to worry about him sleeping with strangers, or getting a blow job in some bathroom.

I have never wanted to be straight. But I don't always want to be gay. It's such hard work some-times. How would I ever explain to my parents that Daniel belongs to a jerk-off club? How could I ever convince them what a good thing it is for him?

Andrea must be a miracle worker. She and the Blue Lady have almost convinced me to just forget about this club. But Saturday is just a few days off. How will I ever get through that night?

Maybe Daniel and I don't walk hand in hand down the street. But he kisses me in public. In the subway station, in movie theatres, in front of the Plaza hotel. He has never been afraid to kiss me in public. If anyone is ever a little hesitant, it's me. I sometimes imagine that after we kiss, some thug will come up and punch us. But no one has ever tried anything like that. And even if he did, we'd have each other to defend us.

"WHAT ARE YOU making such a big deal about? A bunch of guys pulling on each other's puds in a bar. So what?"

I am sitting on Randy's couch. He is polishing the dining room table.

"But it hurts me. It makes me feel as if I'm not . . . as if I'm a loser."

"I told you never to say that about yourself again. It's that repressed Catholic upbringing of yours. The Catholics teach you to hate yourself. Especially if you're queer." He places the vase of orchids back in the center of the table.

"It's just sex. It has nothing to do with you. It's a sport, like bowling. Since faggots are no good at sports, we have sex instead."

I help him move the dining room table away from the mirror, so he can polish its brass frame.

"What if he leaves me?"

"What if he leaves you? You'll survive. Do you think he's the only man around? You're young, you're hot. I bet if you went to that club, you'd be a star."

"Do you really think so?"

"Of course. I went to one of those places once. It was pretty much what you'd expect: all the guys with the big ones were in one group, and the guys with the little ones were in another. I was too embarrassed to do anything. God, I hate this mirror."

Randy works the polish into the tiny grooves of the frame. The mirror was a present from Brian's mother. Otherwise, it would be in the garbage.

I sit back down on the couch.

"I've thought about this a long time. I could stop seeing him if I wanted to. But I don't. I care about him too much."

Randy throws the dirty polishing rag down to the floor.

"Why don't you just admit it? You're looking for an excuse to end the relationship."

That isn't true. Oh God, that isn't true. I don't want to stop seeing him.

"That's what all this garbage is about, isn't it? 'I'm a loser, nobody wants me.' Why don't you just admit you'd rather be alone?"

"That isn't true."

"Oh, come on. If it weren't the jerk-off club, it would be something else."

"You're wrong. I've working a long time at getting to know him. I didn't call him too much right away, I never said a word about fidelity, I didn't tell him I wanted to get married."

"Thank God for that. You're queer. Queers don't get married to each other."

"I know that. I *do* want to be with him. I care for him very much. But I can't be perfect. I just need some time to get used to the idea of this club."

"This has something to do with your parents, doesn't it? With the fact that your father never cheated on your mother, even while she was in the hospital. Have you ever thought of how it affected him, to be stuck with three kids at his age? Maybe he should've gone out and gotten his rocks off."

"My father would never betray my mother like that."

"Betray. Listen to that word. I think you better talk to your therapist about this."

"I already have. You just can't understand someone being faithful. Because you and Brian can't be faithful to each other."

"We don't need to be faithful; we don't even

have sex anymore."

He picks the rag back up off the floor and continues polishing the mirror. I'm afraid I have said too much. But he's hurt my feelings, too. I walk over to the mirror, link my arms around his waist.

"I'm sure Brian still wants you. He just needs to talk to somebody."

DANIEL IS ASLEEP on his back. He is snoring lightly. I am staring at his bedroom ceiling.

Thursday. Two days until this party. What am I going to do? I can't talk about it anymore. I've already said too much. He can probably sense that I don't want him to go. But I *do* want him to go. I mean, I want him to feel free to do what he wants. I wish I could get my face to say "yes." Randy says that even if I tell him it's all right that he goes, my face will be saying "no." How do I stop my face from talking?

Think about the Blue Lady. Think about what she is teaching you. "How much room?" I want my heart to be big, big enough to understand many things. Maybe when my heart is big enough, her fingers will have more room. Maybe then they won't hurt so much, poking around inside me.

I roll over on my stomach. A postcard, the dining room of a hotel, sits on the bed's headboard. Should I read it? He's asleep, he'll never know. Andrea would say it is not a good idea. If you act like you don't trust him, you'll feel like you don't trust him. I trust him. But I still want to read the postcard.

"Dear D.,

I so much enjoyed our recent lunch. The peaches melba were delicious. It's too bad you declined my invitation to dinner. You could have met P.L.'s daughter. What do you think it means, that your initials are the same as my parents' diamond mine? Only the future knows.

Sincerely,

J.J.

Who is J.J.? I don't dare ask him. All he'd need is to know that I'm reading his mail. I don't think I like this J.J. person. What if Daniel is having an affair?

Andrea was right; already you are beginning to mistrust him. Why did I read the stupid card? Well, if he's having an affair, there's nothing you can do about it. You can't trick him into choosing you. You are going to spend the rest of your life torturing yourself, alternating between worrying about his club and worrying about this J.J.?

The whole thing is ridiculous. He is not having an affair: he is sleeping beside you. And even if he were . . .

I put my arms around him and close my eyes. But for just a few moments, I open my eyes again, and look at his sleeping face.

IT IS SATURDAY NIGHT. I am standing in the doorway of Daniel's bathroom. He is combing his hair in the mirror. I am watching him.

How many men have I watched this way? I see them combing their hair, or shaving. I watch them tying their ties. But they never notice me, watching. And when they look at themselves in the mirror, their faces are so full of being a man. There is that pain, around their eyes, and that terrible fear. They see it in their own reflection. But just for a moment. In those final minutes before they go out into the world, they see the pain. And then they are so easy to love. Then, as I watch them combing their hair, I know why I love men.

"I'm sorry I can't bring you with me," he says, "but the party's for members only. Maybe some time in the future, we can go together."

Oh my God. I never thought that he might actually ask me to go with him to his club.

"That's all right. I'll probably go to a movie with Randy and Brian."

"Would you like to stay here tonight?"

I would like that very much. All week I have been telling myself that everything will be all right. It doesn't matter if he goes to the club, as long as he comes home to me. If I stay here tonight, he will have to come home to me.

"I had a set of keys made for you."

What? He must want them back, tomorrow.

"You can keep them, if you like."

"That would be nice."

I can hear Andrea already: PAY ATTENTION TO THIS. He has just given you a set of his keys. You know how he is about his privacy. He's trying to tell you something. Maybe he can't stop going to his club, but he can give you the keys to his apartment.

What will I do with myself tonight, while he's at his party? I should try and stay out as late as possible. I'll go crazy if I have to sit up all alone, waiting for him. I know I'll imagine the worst things. Maybe Randy and Brian will want to go dancing after the movie. No. Brian doesn't like to dance. He doesn't seem to want to do much of anything lately.

Do I love Daniel? I enjoy the time I spend with him very much. We almost never fight. Whenever there is a disagreement, we manage to work things out. He is always so gentle, so reasonable. But do I love him yet?

I guess I need more time. If I don't love him, I can't imagine what it is I do feel. I have never in my life worked so hard at being with someone. I have never been this tough with myself, not allowing me to give in to all my insecurities, not allowing me to fall in that trap of thinking that my life will be like someone else's.

And I have never once wanted Daniel to save me. I don't need to be saved. And if I did, I could do the saving.

But there is still tonight to get through. I don't

want to be afraid. I want to show him the best parts of me, the parts that believe I am not bad, the parts that are not desperate.

MICHAEL AND I broke up once. That is, once before he left me for good. It was only for about a week or so. Then he came back, and everything was fine. Or so I pretended.

Michael's best friend (aside from his lover back west) was visiting from art school. But since nobody at the school was supposed to know that I even existed, I had to pretend that I was Michael's buddy. I wasn't sure how I was supposed to act; I had never been someone's "buddy" before. I tried to be relaxed, to pretend that Michael and I were casual friends, drinking pals or something. Bill was attractive, dark, with fine features, and very friendly. I had a momentary fantasy of sleeping with him just to prove to Michael how good an actor I really was. But Michael made sure that Bill and I never spent too much time alone together. I grudgingly went along with the charade, but every once in a while, I would slip something into the conversation to let Bill know just what good "friends" Michael and I were, something about how much time we spent together, or about the fact that Michael loved tuna fish sandwiches and snored when he slept on his back and wore plaid boxer shorts.

We walked into a gay bar, the bar where Michael had first seen me, the bar we went to every single night that summer we met. Bill led the way, followed by me, and then Michael. While Bill's head was turned, I reached behind me and grabbed Michael, moving my hand up between his legs. I squeezed his dick just hard enough to irritate him. I suppose it was my way of reminding him how much I resented pretending to be his "friend." He made only the slightest exclamation, so that Bill wouldn't turn around to see what was happening. I glanced back at him, and smiled.

We sat at a small round table, and Michael excused himself to go to the men's room. Bill's eyes followed him to the door.

"I bet Michael feels pretty lonely here," he said.

"Why?" I asked.

"Well, he's here all alone this whole summer while Todd is back home."

"Todd?"

"His lover."

Of course I knew Todd was his lover, even though I almost never said his name. Of course I knew what Bill meant. But I wanted to hear it. I wanted to punish myself for falling in love with the wrong man. It felt good in an ugly sort of way, to say Todd's name, to hear Bill worry about Michael and how lonely he was feeling.

"Yeah, I suppose you're right," I said.

MICHAEL AND I had our worst fight ever the day Bill returned home. Once he was safely on his plane heading west, I telephoned Michael.

I told him that I needed to talk to him right away. He complained that he was tired, that entertaining Bill, being obliged to lie to him about our relationship, had been a strain on him. Finally, he agreed to see me.

I don't remember much of the conversation that night except that I told him I was tired, tired of being the person whose feelings were always considered last, after Todd's, after whoever's feelings Michael was trying to spare by keeping our relationship a secret. He put on his shoes and headed for the door, and I said:

"If you leave now, don't bother coming back," just like I had heard in the movies. And just like in the movies, Michael left.

And for the next week or so, I walked around as if I were in shock. I was interviewed on a local television show about an acting part I was doing, and the whole time, I kept imagining Michael watching me from some far off TV set, with tears in his eyes. I thought I saw his face several times in the crowds I passed while riding the bus. I kept hoping for a telephone call, or a letter, or something. And then one night, I opened the door of my parents' home, hoping that it might be him, Michael, coming to apologize and to promise that things were over once and for all between him and that other person back west. And I opened the door, and there was Michael, and I burst into tears, threw my arms around him and said

"Please, don't ever do that again."

It was just the way I had imagined it to be, the perfect reconciliation. Except that he never said a word to me about the fight. He didn't apologize, and he had no intention of leaving Todd for me. We never, ever, spoke about it again.

I knew something was wrong. I knew that Michael was treating me badly. But I could not bring myself to say anything. I was just so grateful, so relieved that he had actually come back. But something was changed. Even if he *had* come back, and he *was* sleeping beside me again, something inside me was different. It just didn't feel the same, to stare at his face while he slept.

And then, a few months later, Michael left for good. And that was the end of that story.

THIS IS THE NIGHT of the Blue Lady's hands. She entered me slowly tonight, her hands brushing lightly over my breastbone, searching the soft spot, up, between my lungs, her fingers one by one pierced the soft spot under my breastbone, up they reached, past the skin, the muscle, the blood, past my ribs and into my heart.

Knives tonight, her fingers, moving deep inside me. I hug myself, bury my face in my knees. Can my heart be so small? Maybe tonight I will open up like a flower, maybe the touch of her hands will make the rooms of my heart bloom like a flower, maybe her touch will be warmth against my skin, after tonight, my heart full of room, enough to take him in, enough to wrap around him, after tonight, he'll place his hands inside me too, touch the rooms of my heart, and there will be no more pain, there will be no more bleeding.

It is two o'clock. I sit on his bed, counting out the cards, the first one face up, then a row face down, two, three, four, five, six, seven, eight, nine. Another one up, two, three, four, five, six, seven, eight. Another one up, two, three, four, five, six, seven. Another one up, two, three, four, five, six. Another one up, two, three, four, five. Another one up, two, three, four. Another one up, two, three. Another one up, two. Another one up. I hold the remaining cards in my left hand.

Pig, I will say, you disgust me. Leave me alone, leave me, show your dick to someone else, take your filthy body out of my sight.

I pick up the ashtray from the headboard. It is glazed in blue and green, mottled blue and green, and on the bottom, carved in his eight-year-old hand, is his name. Daniel. I press it to my mouth, it feels cool against my lips.

The Blue Lady, I hate her tonight. She is cruel, and her hands are reckless as a child's, moving in and out of my heart, this must be how it feels, to be disemboweled, to stick the knife inside my own stomach, watch the inside spill out, stain the sheets, cover the bed in my blood.

One, two, three, the third card I turn up. Black six on top of red seven. One, two, a red jack.

His beard is red, and he reaches behind him, takes someone's cock in his hand, he spreads his legs, and rubs the head against his ass, someone's cock, he can't see, his face is pressed down into the floor, and

Red jack to the bottom of the pile.

Daniel, I would wipe from your mouth the taste of shame and fear. Let me cover the dark boy, press him against me, put his hands inside me. Show me your mouth when the sun is so bright it amazes you, show me your hands.

Betrayal. Three infant sons. Never. Ever. And when I am sick, who will save me? And when I am desperate and hate myself, who will stop my hands, stop the knife from slitting open the feathery veins, the purple veins?

One, two, I turn up the third card. Red five, the black four, king in the

He stands facing a mirror, and a hand reaches around to touch his nipple, rubs his chest, and down, moves down his stomach, over the hair and

empty space, one, two, three, the ace of hearts above, one, two, three.

Leave him if you like. You have your excuse, the knives, and he will not save you. Nobody will save you.

Tonight I will not move from her. I will remain perfectly still until she is finished, until she is tired of moving in and out of me, tearing me open. I will make no sound from my throat, or cry. I wait for her hands, they move through the rooms, the spaces inside me, touch the bleeding inside me, I

I hear the key turn in the lock. Quickly, I gather the cards in a pile, the lamp, I reach up to turn out the light, and pull the covers up around my naked shoulders.

"HELLO?" He closes the door behind him, peers through the dark, into his bedroom.

"How was your party?" I smile.

"Great. I'm exhausted." He walks to the bed, bends down, and kisses me. I see the boy in the photograph, the clear eyes, the mouth I remember.

When he is lying on his back, my arm across his chest, I can feel his heartbeat, there is almost nothing I am afraid to ask him.

"Is it like us?" My mouth is near his ear, my lips touch his ear.

"What?"

"Is what you do at your club like what happens with us?"

But I know how he will answer me; I know it, and still I ask.

"No, nothing at all. It's kind of a game. You try and see how excited you can get the other men. It's a performance. Like acting."

Do you act with me? No. I remember. Is this the time? I'm not afraid, I can say it, I can say those words and know that I'm not desperate. She was wrong, I am not a child, or poison, or

"Would you like to go with me next week? I can bring a guest."

Oh God, wait, don't say anything stupid or crazy
or panic.

"I'd have to think about it. I'd have to hear
much more about it."

I AM RUNNING A MILE.

The sun is so bright, it hurts my eyes, and the
fence around the track makes me feel as if I'm in prison. My arms and legs, I'm ashamed, the sticks hanging from the sleeves of my yellowed tee shirt, the torn
green shorts. My jock pinches my skin. From what
will it protect me?

We are the last four. I don't remember them,
the sun is so bright I can't see their faces, but I can
guess how they look: bad skin, spindly arms and legs,
glasses, braces, they are too tall or too short or too
fat or too thin or too dumb or too smart or too quiet
or too loud or too

The coach's hand hangs in the air, his stop
watch, his clipboard. His face, a skull, the brown
parchment skin stretched tight across it. I could
leave. I could walk right off the track, back into the
locker room.

His hand cuts the air like a knife, and we run,
we are afraid, but more afraid of the shame of fear,
we run, and the wind in our legs, blowing up our
shorts, across our naked asses, the wind in our faces,
blowing our hair, we forget the fear, feel the sun on
our skin, the reckless wind, my hurt, the sun is so
bright I can taste it, we circle around the track.

HOW DO I refuse him? At least if I go with him to the club, we'll be together. I have not been naked in front of more than one man since my high school gym class.

"Do you touch other men?"

"Yes. Sometimes."

Seeing him touch someone else, seeing the pleasure on his face, the face that looks up at me from beneath my body? No. I would leave the room, he would be embarrassed, uncomfortable. Or I would touch someone else, lose my pain in another man's body, prove to him that I can, and then feel the pleasure of jealousy, his jealousy.

I AM RUNNING.

The muscles of my legs grip, and every step, my head throbs. Air is poison, my lungs fill with poison, they spit out the air, the sun is so bright I can't see, I want to stop, I want to leave, step out of this prison, but I am afraid of the shame, my legs kick the dirt, my mouth is like sand, I see the brown skull floating ahead of me, I know it is almost over, almost over.

"IT'S FRATERNAL. It's a way for men to express their sexuality in a free and open way. Lots of guys do it as children, and they're not just gay. Why should they stop when they're older?"

Male bonding. He reminds me of Randy, and

his bisexual rap group. Belonging, feeling the sensuality of being in a group of men together, naked, hot. And still I would be an outsider. Jesus, I'm a man. I have never wanted to be anything but a man. But I've never felt as if I belonged with men. I always thought that the reason I fell in love with men was because I wasn't like them. Maybe all those years of telling myself I was like my mother.

"You are not like your mother."

Andrea is wearing her purple dress, the dress I like so much. I want to tell her how pretty she looks, but I am afraid. We never talk about her. Three years of seeing her every week, and I know so little about her.

"Nervous breakdowns are not contagious. Just because she had one doesn't mean you will too."

I don't need to be saved. And if I did, I would save myself.

But if I am not like her, I am also not like him.

"Is it a kind of betrayal, to admit that your life can't be like theirs?"

MY HEAD hangs over my legs, my legs have stopped, we are finished, but the air is still poison, my body spits out the poison, I feel my blood flowing down, away from my eyes, I see yellow, the air is yellow, my spit flows down my throat, everything down inside my stomach, I have finished, there is no more fear of shame, but the poison flows down into my stomach, the yellow, my face turns yellow, I hug myself, and the poison spurts up, out of my throat, all over the locker room floor.

Quickly, I wipe up the vomit. No one sees me. No one will ever know. I will not be ashamed.

"I'VE THOUGHT about this for a long time, and I don't think I should go to your club."

We are lying in bed, after making love. My arm is stretched across his chest. I am not afraid.

"I don't think you'd have a good time if I were there."

"Why is that?"

"Because if I saw you touch another man, I'd have to come over and break your ribs. And I know you wouldn't like that."

He laughs, and kisses my forehead.

ANDREA AGREES it is not a good idea for me to go to his club. She says the memories will stay in my head, make pictures, pictures that will resurface when I least expect it, when I'm making love with him, when I am afraid.

And I don't really want to go. Not because of what Randy says, about how I'm repressed, or too uptight, or riddled with Catholic guilt. Everyone has a right to determine what role sex will play in his life. Even me. I don't want it to be a sport. I hate sports. I always have.

This is one time when I can't escape the Blue

Lady's fingers. I will always be afraid of this club, afraid that I may lose him to it, afraid of how it will affect him. But my heart is big enough. There is room enough to allow for this club. I have no need to be ashamed of my heart.

MANY TIMES, growing up, I was mistaken for a girl. It started as long ago as I can remember, and continued even up until the time I was in high school. It was a constant source of pain and embarrassment for me, one of the things I was most ashamed of about myself.

I never understood how it happened. I tried to look like other boys. I dressed in dark colors, browns and blues. I tried to speak loudly. My skin was so smooth, I rubbed dirt on it to make it look rough and scraped, as if I had been playing football or something. But nothing seemed to work.

I suppose it was a combination of things: my 1970s long hair, my small stature, my shyness. And it happened in all kinds of different situations — at school, in the supermarket, in church. After a while, I almost got used to it. It was something I anticipated with dread every time I met someone new. Time would pass, and it wouldn't happen for a while, and I would relax a little and think maybe I had outgrown whatever it was that caused people to mistake me for female. Then, when I was least expecting it, it would happen again. It was like being punched in the stomach with shame, like being hit over the head with the fact that something was terribly wrong with me.

I felt like a freak. I felt as if I wanted to disappear. My only consolation was the fact that I knew, one day, I would be able to grow a moustache or a beard, and then, the whole terrible thing would be over with once and for all.

I have heard some other people talk about the pain they felt as a child, being mistaken for a member of the opposite sex. What amazes me most about it is the feeling of shame. I wonder why it should feel so horrible, to be called "she" instead of "he." I'm sure it is difficult for little girls who are mistaken for boys, but somehow, it seems worse for males. Or maybe it is just that women seem to be able to laugh about it when they are adults, while men still feel some of the residual shame. They are not so eager to speak about the experience. Even after all these years, it is still difficult for me to admit that I was sometimes mistaken for a girl. I know I didn't do anything wrong, anything to deserve what happened. But I feel as if I should be ashamed, as if I should be reluctant to admit what happened.

I AM RIDING in the front seat of my parents' car, I must be maybe six or seven years old, and we are downtown, driving past the porno theaters, the book-stores, and I am crying, and there is that terrible feeling in my stomach, the hollow pain that stretches down from my ribs to my feet, my head, I lie down on the seat of the car, and I am crying, between my mother and father, they don't understand, I see the pictures, the ads for the live sex shows, the women with chains around their necks, like dog collars, the men with their faces covered in black leather hoods, and I am afraid, they said sex was love, the beautiful thing that happened between two people when they loved each other, and I am confused, and I cry, and I feel myself slipping inside me, falling into the space, the hollow that stretches from my ribs down to my feet, my stomach, and my parents don't understand, and they are afraid for me, and later, years, I don't understand this horrible fear, being lost, abandoned, with nothing to hold, slipping inside myself, and no one to hold me when I am afraid, and no one to touch the tears as they fall from my face.

My poems make it so much easier to say the things I am afraid to say in real life. It hurts so much less, to tell a story.

DINNER AFTER THERAPY

Dying petals drip
in the white candle heat,
yellowed falling fingers
crumpled with sickness
remind me of days
when that terror of boredom
twisted me up,

sent me to bed
in the middle of the day,
dreaming of sleep.
You touch my hand
across the table.
The doctor's voice
pronounces in my memory
its Berlitz recording
of symptoms and
this is wrong
I think, I am well,
and move myself down deep
in your animal eyes
and imagine your mouth on mine.
The doctor's voice
repeats its warning
and leaves fall down
to the plates like litter
and I remember nights
you pulled me up
against your,
pressed my face to your
chest and
fear fell away
like the sweaters
we tossed to the floor,
clothes we tore off
as if they were the walls
coming between us
instead of this slow disease
folding me up inside myself,
turning my speech to wood.

WE ARE SITTING at the piano bench, our legs lightly
brushing against each other, I can feel his leg against

mine through his pants. He sings *"Mi fai dimenticare Iddio"* and I stop playing the piano and place my hands against his breastbone, feel the sound, the richness of the sound that fills the room.

He sings and I remember, the Blue Lady, the dark boy who smiles at me from the photograph, the photograph I carry with me now. He opens up like a flower. He can't see it; it happens almost against his will, the richness of his voice bursts his body open, and the sound is like water, covers me over, fills the room. There are no words to describe his voice and how it tells the story of his life, all the things he cannot say, every moment he has ever lived. He sings, and I see only him.

He reaches into his pocket, pulling out a plain gold band. He places the ring on my middle finger.

"I'd like to let you keep it, but it was a present to me from my father. You can wear it though, if you like."

Is this the time? He is so gentle. No, don't speak just yet. Take his hands. I press them against my chest in the soft spot beneath my breastbone. Then I move them to my heart, let him feel the even beating.

I WRITE A POEM about Daniel. Even in the poem, I try not to say too much. I imagine that I am St. Francis of Assisi, and he is someone I am trying not to scare away, someone who isn't yet sure that it is safe to be with me. I call the poem "Young Francis in Love." I

wish I could be as careful in life as I am in my
poems.

YOUNG FRANCIS IN LOVE

"Sparrows, your hands
brush their feathers against my face,
light on my lips, then disappear,
fly south, to sleep safe,
safe in your warm winter pockets.

"Such shy birds, how
shall I lead them
to their new home
on my shoulders, my neck,
how may I bring them
back up north
to spend a season
asleep on my skin.

"Shall I shave my head,
beg for bread,
talk to leaves?

"Would madness allow
a humbled heart
to change its rhythm
to beating of wings,

"Convince the creatures
no cage will
close its bars
around their wintry dreams?"

"IT's ONLY NATURAL, for men to want to have sex with more than one partner. Even if you have a lover. If some hot-looking guy were cruising you, I'm sure you'd want to follow him home. Even if you didn't let yourself."

Brian, Randy, Daniel, and I. We are eating dinner, at a restaurant. I don't want to have this discussion. Not in front of Daniel. Not before we've talked about it privately.

Monogamy, fidelity. I have never mentioned those words. I do not want to be forced into saying certain things in front of Daniel. Not just yet, before we've had the time to discuss it. The Blue Lady's fingers, I

"Arguing about what's *natural* is pretty pointless. How will we ever know how much of what we do is 'natural' and how much is learned?"

"Oh, come on. That's just semantics. It's natural to feel sexual."

"Yeah, you see somebody hot, and your dick gets hard. That's natural."

"Don't you feel a little funny, being gay and using the word 'natural'? Who decides what's natural and what isn't? There are plenty of people who would call us unnatural."

"If it happens, it's natural, as far as I'm concerned."

"And it's natural for men to be attracted to people other than their lovers."

"I don't agree. I don't . . . when I'm in love with

someone, I'm not really attracted to other men. Does that make me 'unnatural'?"

"You would be attracted to them, if you weren't so uptight. If your parents hadn't taught you that it was immoral."

"That's bullshit. And even if it were true, are we supposed to act on everything we feel? Maybe it's 'natural' for me to want to kill you if you make me angry. But that doesn't mean I'm going to do it."

"There is no comparison, between having sex with someone and killing him. That's a ridiculous analogy."

"No it isn't. Look, when I'm in love with someone, I'm not attracted to other people. I'm just not. I don't know why, but it just doesn't happen to me."

"That is unnatural. Look at the history of marriage. It's the result of religion and economics. Lots of other cultures don't insist on monogamy. It's only because of those nasty Catholics that people are monogamous today."

"The Arabs had lots of wives."

"What does that have to do with us?"

"Have you ever studied the history of marriage?"

"No, but. . ."

"Have you ever studied the history of marriage? You don't know what you're talking about."

"Why is it okay for everyone to choose what he wants to do with his body, except me? If I choose monogamy, then I'm unnatural. It isn't fair."

"See, you just admitted it. You *choose* monogamy. No matter what you choose, the urge is still there, to fuck some other guy."

"But that's not how I feel. I don't. I don't believe this. I was told when I was younger that being gay was unnatural. Now I'm told by other men that I'm unnatural because I don't want to sleep around. I'm so tired of having this same fight over and over again with the two of you."

"Why don't you just admit it; it's because of your parents. You idolized their relationship. You thought they were perfect."

Three infant sons, a nervous breakdown, no, that isn't fair, I don't believe that anymore.

"Why don't *you* admit that you can't be monogamous? It's because of your repressed, closeted upbringing."

"That's not true."

"Yes it is."

"Look at history. We're not supposed to be with just one person. Being gay means no rules. Besides, if you're a healthy man, you enjoy having sex with many partners. It's fun. If it weren't for women, straight men would be acting just like us. There would be no such thing as monogamy."

"What does history have to do with anything? People have always killed each other. Does that make it something we should continue to do?"

"Calm down."

"There you go again with that killing business. Why are you so judgmental? Sex isn't love. It's whatever you want it to be."

"I don't believe that."

"Well that's your problem."

"It's not that simple."

"Why? Because of morality?"

"No. It has nothing to do with morality. If you behave a certain way for a long time, it affects you. If you act like sex is dirty, then you start to feel like sex is dirty."

"Who said anything about sex being dirty? You're just afraid of your own sexual feelings."

"All right, I admit 'dirty' is the wrong word. But if you act ashamed . . ."

"Who's ashamed?"

"You don't think having sex in bathrooms or dark bars is acting like you're ashamed?"

"No. It's hot. Hot, raw, sex. And only sex. It's fun. It's a sport."

"Well I don't want sex to be something I do with strangers. I want it to be something I share with the person I love."

"Why can't it be both, one way with your lover, and another with someone else?"

"Because people aren't that way."

"That's your judgment."

"No it's not. Psychologically, people can't do it."

"You're wrong. That's just your opinion."

"No it isn't. Look, if I see a black cat on the sidewalk in front of me, and I cross the street because I am afraid, then I've acted on that feeling of fear. And my fear of black cats increases. It has nothing to do with morality. It's a question of human behavior."

"What are you talking about? What does a black

cat have to do with anything?"

"If you act like sex is something you do with strangers, then those feelings become attached to that act. And you end up not wanting to have sex with the person you love."

"That's bullshit. You're wrong. Sex can be many things. You're just too judgmental. Why can't you allow other people to do whatever they want with their bodies?"

"I'm not judgmental. You started this argument, Brian, by saying that I'm unnatural because I'm not like you."

"I think we're making a scene."

"Am I too loud?"

"No, but you're awfully defensive."

"It's because I'm so tired of this argument. Why don't we just admit we each have our own very subjective perspectives. This discussion amounts to fighting for our lives."

"What are you talking about?"

"Every time we have this argument, we try and defend the way we've lived our whole lives. None of us are objective. I am the way I am because I don't know how to live any other way. And you don't know any way but your way. Maybe it's the differences in our ages."

"What do you mean?"

"My friends didn't grow up having sex in bathrooms with strangers. We wanted to take our boyfriends home for Sunday dinner with the family. It's different now. Because of AIDS, because of other things too, different attitudes. I always wanted to fall in love with another man. I don't know why."

"I don't agree. I know plenty of younger guys who aren't monogamous or in relationships. And you can be in love with someone and still have sex with other men."

"I don't believe it. I mean, I don't want my life to be like that."

"Why not? What are you afraid of? You're not your parents; you're gay."

"I don't want to be like them."

"Oh yes you do."

"I do not."

"Maybe we should talk about something else," says Daniel.

RANDY CALLS ME on the telephone a few days later.

"I'm sorry. I know we shouldn't have had that argument in front of Daniel. We were a little rough on you."

"It's all right."

"I could tell you were upset by the look on your face. As soon as Brian brought it up, you got this look on your face like you'd rather be talking about anything else but sex. I hope you're not upset."

"That's all right. I didn't say anything I prob- ably wouldn't say again."

But I am upset. I shouldn't have let Daniel hear some of the things I was saying. Not just yet. It is too soon to start talking about fidelity or monogamy.

And it wasn't a fair fight. Brian and Randy used all the ammunition they could, everything they knew about my life, everything I've told them. But I couldn't do that to them. I couldn't say, look at your own lives. You love each other, but you can't sleep together. All those years, the Meat Rack, the balcony at the Saint, the men's rooms.

But I couldn't say that. Randy would have said that it was all Brian's fault, that *he* was more than willing to have sex. Brian would have been hurt and embarrassed. I love them both too much, even with all the fighting, to say those things.

It's not Randy I am afraid of hurting. He is strong. But Brian. He pretends to be so uncaring, so unafraid. But inside, I know he is just a baby, lonely, needing to be loved. They are so lucky to have each other.

"I'M SORRY you had to hear that argument between Randy and Brian and me."

We are sitting at his kitchen table after making love. Both of us are still naked. I am holding the fingers of his right hand, pulling them as I speak. The breakfast dishes, smeared with the last of the scrambled eggs, are pushed to the center of the table.

"Monogamy doesn't really matter all that much to me. What matters most is what happens between the two of us."

He smiles. His hair is sticking up around his ears, it makes little wings, reminds me of a little boy's.

"The important thing is that we talk to each other. As long as we keep talking to each other, we'll be fine."

He brushes the hair on my right arm with his free hand.

"But sometimes people do things they're ashamed of, things they'd prefer not to talk about," he says.

I want to say, there is nothing you could possibly tell me that would make me think less of you. I want to say, we can work out anything, if we talk about it.

But I don't say a word.

"Dear D.,

My self respect is fading fast. All I have is that memory of our first meeting, the lunch, the dessert, peaches melba. October _____, I wrote down the date so I will always remember. Why has fate allowed our paths to cross? Only time will tell. In the meantime, I dream of the future.

J.J."

Why does he leave his mail lying around? He knows I have keys to his apartment. It is torture for me, to find this second postcard. I have a desperate urge to search his drawers while he is in the bathroom. But I will not allow myself to behave that way. If I wait patiently enough, he will tell me about this J.J., and his postcards. He has never lied to me. And even if he were seeing someone else, what could I do?

I won't be involved in a contest to "win him" away
from this other person.

Wait. The only thing I can do is wait. I trust
him. I must act like I trust him.

THINGS WITH MICHAEL got really terrible near the
end. I would wait all night long for him to call, and
then when he wouldn't, I would go to bed. My
parents didn't understand what was wrong. I told
them I was tired of disco music. I guess they were so
relieved that I wasn't going to gay bars any more that
they didn't really care to know why.

Some nights, Michael would show up at my
parents' house at around three in the morning. He
would throw rocks at my window to wake me up, and
I would let him in the back door. If he had been
drinking, I would have to get him a glass of water, a
slice of bread, and three aspirins.

"Where were you tonight?"

"I'm not telling."

"We were supposed to have dinner together. I
waited here all night for you."

"I'm sorry."

"It was really embarrassing. My parents kept
looking at me funny, wondering why I was so dressed
up just to watch TV."

"I said I was sorry. What do you want me to do?
Don't make such a big deal out of nothing."

Then he would roll over and go to sleep. Once,
I even found him passed out in his car. He was

parked right in front of my parents' driveway, and he had thrown up all over the floor of the car.

"Oh, I guess he's still depressed about his best friend committing suicide," I told my parents.

But the really horrible thing, worse than the puking and the fighting and the hours of waiting by the telephone, was the fact that I thought it was all just the way it was supposed to be. Even passed out in the car, and standing me up, and hardly ever telling me that he loved me, he was still the man of my dreams. I honestly thought that all of those things were just part of being in love. And for some reason, it always seemed as if I got just what I deserved. I know it is another one of those things that does and doesn't make sense.

"So, how are things going?" she asks.

I never believed I would love another man. After Michael. My parents fell in love once, and lived happily ever after. Maybe I couldn't live happily ever after with Michael. But I could make sure I never loved anyone else.

I pretended as if I wanted to meet someone and fall in love. I dated many different men. But always men who could never love me, men whom I could never love. We tortured each other, argued, complained about each other's habits, sometimes even cheated on each other, until it became painfully apparent to both of us that things couldn't go on. It was an ideal arrangement. I got and gave them sex, and kept myself busy. But I knew I'd never fall in love with any of them. No matter how much I pretended. The only ones I ever truly cared about were the ones who were too afraid to love me.

But that is all over now, that was before. It was almost an accident, that Daniel and I fell in love. Or so it seems. And now I want to tell him.

"I want to tell him that I love him. But I am afraid."

The box of tissues sits dangerously close to me today. Andrea knows that something is wrong. She can always tell. She'll ask me questions, and we'll talk, but I won't be able to say what I need to say, and I will become more frustrated, and feel the sadness rising up from my stomach, up to my face, into my throat. And then somehow she will say the right thing, a word, a question, a phrase, and the sadness will break out of me, fill my eyes, and I'll cry, and it will feel warm and safe, to push this sadness out of my stomach, to feel the warmth of my tears on my face, to wrap myself in the sadness.

"What are you afraid of?"

"I'm afraid he'll find out that I love him too much."

I AM SITTING on Randy's couch. His arms are around me, he strokes my hair, brushes away the hair from my face, the ugly, crying face, the face that I am embarrassed to show him.

"Daniel won't leave you because you love him

too much." He is speaking softly, his mouth feels warm against my ear. He laughs, a quiet laugh. "God, do you know what I'd do, if Brian told me he loved me too much? I'd get down on my knees, and thank God. Honestly. I would be ecstatic, if Brian told me he was afraid he loved me too much."

THE SADNESS is still lodged in my stomach. I am impatient with her today. She is taking her time, it is difficult for her to find those words which will open me up, send the pain breaking out of me.

The warm tears roll down my face and I cry, silently. I reach for a tissue from the box on the table. For a moment, I lose myself in the sadness. I stare down at the pink marble table.

I AM FIVE, I am six, I am seven years old, and Momma, I love you so much it hurts, whenever I tell you, I start to cry, and mornings, your pink flannel nightgown, and I am afraid, I am leaving for school, I kiss you goodbye and you shake, you shake, you shake so badly I am afraid your body is breaking and it is my fault, I am bad I am bad, and at night before going to sleep, your nightgown, I love you so much, I run to kiss you goodnight, and as my arms link around your neck to hug you, you shake, you shake so much I can barely hang on to you and it is my fault, I am bad, what have I done, to make my mother shake like a puppet whenever I kiss her, my love is bad, it will send her away from me, back to the hospital, back to the man with the awful machine that will make her forget her name, her husband, her sons. I am bad. I am bad.

YEARS, THE FEAR would seize me, the feeling of being lost, abandoned, and wanting to die, to kill myself to avoid the horrible fear, and always as the sadness spewed out like poison from my stomach, I would hug myself and ask, what have I done, God forgive me, I will do anything you ask, please take this away, this fear that would cause me to kill myself to escape it. And I would hate myself. Because deep down, I would know that I had done something to deserve this punishment. Somehow, I must in some way be responsible for this pain.

"YOU DIDN'T CAUSE your mother's sickness by loving her too much. It had nothing to do with you. You know that."

But when you love someone too much, they leave you. It happened with my mother. It happened with Michael, and it will probably happen with Daniel, too.

"So what about the people you love who haven't left you? What about your father, what about your brothers, what about Randy and Brian? Or don't you love them?"

Of course I love them. Of course it doesn't make

sense, to believe that loving someone will drive them away from you. But it feels true, inside me, in that bad part of me that wants to believe that I have done something to deserve this pain.

"We all want the world to make sense. When we are children, our parents always tell us that everything will be all right. So when something happens that doesn't make sense, that can't be made 'right' with a kiss or a hug, then we tell ourselves a story. We make up a reason, find some reason for why things happen the way they do. That way, the world will still make sense. It doesn't make sense, for your mother to leave you when you are only two years old. So you decided that it had to be your fault. In that way, you could still have some control over the situation. If your mother left you because you were bad, then being good could make her come back."

A story. Like the story of why Michael left. Like the story of Electric Louie. Like the story of the Blue Lady's hands?

"You want to stop feeling as if your love is poison? If you want to stop feeling as if your love drives people away, then don't act on that feeling. Tell Daniel you love him. You need to know that he will not leave you if you love him too much, because you love him too much. You aren't bad. There is nothing wrong with your love.

"And if he does leave you, you need to know that, too."

I AM RIDING the subway this cold December morning. It is so cold, no one bothers to remove their gloves, even inside the car. I take a seat near the door.

"Hey babe, how ya doin'?"

Out of the corner of my eye, I see a black man. Was he speaking to me? He wears heavy boots and brown suede gloves, a long black coat, and a black fur hat. He looks to be about fifty or so, and hasn't shaved in several days. He is speaking rapidly, mumbling in a low growl. The seat beside him is empty.

"Hey babe, how ya doin'?"

Every time someone new gets on the car, male or female, he greets them this way. Otherwise, he continues to mumble a stream of unintelligible growls. People around him look uptight; they are afraid of him, or at least annoyed. Someone sits down beside him, a Korean woman, her arms loaded with plastic bags full of groceries. He begins talking to her, I can't make out the words. She gets up, moves to another part of the train.

The train fills up with people, but the seat beside him remains empty. Sometimes, someone will sit down beside him for a moment, until he speaks to them. Once they realize he won't stop talking, they move to another seat.

I watch the other passengers stare at him from over the tops of their newspapers, from behind their magazines. They are trying to guess what is wrong with him. They are all so curious. But if he catches them looking, he'll talk to them, ask them how they are.

"Hey babe, how ya' doin'?"

And so they carefully dodge his glance. What does he want, I wonder. Is he crazy, or lonely, or drunk?

A woman sits down beside him, a black woman in her twenties. She wears jeans, a short wool jacket, and a black floppy hat.

"Hey babe, how ya doin'?"

"Fine thank you. How are you?" she asks him.

They are speaking now, I can't hear the words. What do I hear? He rocks in his seat as he talks, and some of the words make sense, his name is John, what is her name? Mary, something about children, a farm, could he borrow a cigarette?

Mary opens a blue-and-white pack of cigarettes, and hands him three. He removes one of his gloves, and takes the cigarettes. She gives him something else, a small piece of paper.

"Keep the matches," she says.

He lights up the cigarette, smokes with his ungloved hand. The other passengers are annoyed; smoking isn't allowed on the train. His fingers shake as he holds the cigarette to his lips. A man stands near him, then moves away, mumbling something under his breath, something about a smokestack.

Mary gets up from her seat; it is her stop.

"Now don't you forget what I told you, babe. Have a good day."

What did he tell her? What did I miss?

"You too, John."

She leaves the train. Once again, he greets each new passenger.

"Hey babe, how ya doin'?"

He talks to himself, his growl is a continuous stream of sounds. Two stops after Mary's, he rises up out of his seat, and offers it to a young woman. He steps off the train. I can feel the other passengers' relief as he walks onto the subway platform.

All he wanted was to talk to somebody.

I FEEL GUILTY sometimes about Michael. I feel as if I should remember more about the good times, about how it wasn't all terrible. About how it was one of the most beautiful things that ever happened to me. It gets so confusing. The way I tell the story changes all the time. At first, while it was happening, it was wonderful. I wrote down every word so that I would never forget exactly how it happened. I remember how lonely I felt before we met, and how amazing it was to be kissed by a man, and told that you are loved. And sex was better than anything in the world, better than food, better than acting, better than writing poems.

And then, at the end, the story was awful, a terrible dream, a punishment, something I never understood, but somehow felt I deserved. And sex was humiliating, the thing he withheld from me, to make me feel ugly, or stupid, or unloved. And the more he said no, the more I wanted him, and the more he refused, and the more I wanted.

And now, it is like a painting which has only been partially painted over, and I see both scenes at the same time, the good and the bad. All the things that ever happened remain inside me, and I hear them talking, all at the very same time.

But even that is changing. Now, as Daniel and I become closer, the story of Michael disappears, or maybe it becomes just a story, like something I am reading, something that happened to somebody else. I am no longer afraid to throw away scraps of paper on which he had written, the matchbooks from the restaurants where we ate, the cocktail napkins. I know that whatever I want to remember will always be with me. And I don't intend to treat Daniel as if everything he touches belongs in some personal, private museum dedicated to him.

THE GREEN AND SALMON colored rug is rolled up for the night, and the bleached oak floor shines beneath the feet of the guests. Randy and Brian's apartment is decorated with white candles and fresh flowers, orchids and orange gladiolas, and soft music plays on the stereo. I watch Daniel in the brass framed mirror, look over his shoulder, I see our reflection, my hand at the back of his neck, his hair, the shape of his shoulders beneath his shirt, his back, his legs. And I see my own face smile back at me.

It is New Year's Eve. We are dancing. His arms are linked around my waist. My right hand holds him, touches his head, pulls his face closer to mine. I brush my face against his, kiss his cheek. My left hand rests on his shoulder.

I will tell him tonight. At twelve midnight, amid all the confusion and celebrating, I will tell him that I love him. I will find out how it feels, to be the first person to say those words. "I love you."

I wonder how he will react. So much time has been spent making my decision—should I, shouldn't I, is this the right time, the right date—that I haven't given much thought to how he will react. He'll probably just smile.

"You're only saying that to annoy me."

No. He won't say that. He isn't Michael, and I'm not seventeen.

Michael, I see you tonight in my mind, you are combing the hair of someone young, someone who adores you. You straighten his collar, and kiss him on the forehead.

"Remember to stand up straight," you tell him. And he would do anything you asked.

Michael, when we danced, then you had no answers. You didn't want to look like a fool. You were so afraid. But once you had had enough to drink, you never refused me, the tenderness inside you broke free and you grabbed me tight around my waist, you held me against your chest and spun me, laughing, and we'd kick someone and apologize, but keep on dancing.

Dancing with men. What would we do without dancing? I have seen more tenderness between men on a dance floor than almost anywhere else in the world.

"I feel like I'm in high school," I whisper to Daniel, and he laughs, softly.

Brian and Randy are dancing together. I see them across the room. Brian's back is to me, his head rests on Randy's shoulder. I wonder how Randy got him to dance? It is New Year's Eve. Maybe on this one night, Brian will allow himself to be loved.

The song ends, and Daniel leaves to get me a glass of wine. I walk over to Randy and Brian, we sit down on the couch. Daniel joins us.

"It's so nice to see you two dancing," I say.

"He forced me."

"Oh, be quiet."

"He said he'd throw me out of my own party if I didn't dance with him."

"Well, I'm glad," I laugh.

IT IS ALMOST MIDNIGHT, we are dancing again. I link my arms around his neck. Randy and Brian stand nearby.

"Who's gonna get it tonight?" asks Randy.

"I don't know what you're talking about," I say.

"Come one, tell us which one of you gets fucked tonight."

"I don't *believe* you."

"You tell us, and we'll tell you," says Daniel.

"Oh, that's easy. Neither one. Brian gets a headache and goes to sleep."

"Very funny. I'll remember that later," says Brian.

FROM THE WINDOW of their apartment we can see Times Square, the crowd. We are waiting for the ball to drop.

This is the night. I can already feel the Blue Lady's hands. They rest against my chest, feel the beating of my heart. They are warm tonight. Will her fingers enter me, pierce my skin, move in and out of me?

I will tell him. For me. For us. I will not be afraid. I am not desperate.

The voices around me begin to count

Ten, nine, eight,

His arms around me,

seven, six,

we watch the ball,

five, four,

I join with the other voices,

three, two, one,

"Happy New Year," we all yell together. There is "Auld Lang Syne" blaring from the stereo. We see the people below us, waving their arms. He turns to me.

"Happy New Year," he kisses me on the mouth.

"Happy New Year."

I touch his face, his cheek, I move my mouth to his ear, now, I will do it now, I speak it softly in his ear.

"I love you, Daniel."

"I love you, too."

The Blue Lady's fingers, but this time, there is almost no pain. Her hands are inside me, his hands are inside me, the rooms of my heart bloom like a flower, I hug him to me, pull him up against my chest. For the next few moments, there are no voices. Only the sound of my heart opening up at the touch of the Blue Lady's hands.

LATER THAT NIGHT, after making love, we are lying in his bed. I am on top of him, playing with his mouth. My fingers trace the shape of his lower lip.

"I told my father about you today," he whispers.

His father is seventy-five. He is sick, with cancer. He probably won't live too much longer.

"I called him to wish him a Happy New Year. He asked me again about getting married. I told him I was seeing you."

I have never met his parents. They've known he is gay for a few years now. He loves them both very much.

"I love you too."

I hear him say it on the phone to them all the time.

"How did your father react?"

"He said he might like to meet you sometime."

His eyes fill with tears, and he cries, but without a sound. Daniel, in this way, you are like Michael. I have almost never seen you cry. Except when we are in bed together. And always, without a sound.

I kiss his cheek, I wipe his eyes, I brush my face against his.

I AM STANDING on the corner of 59th Street and Lexington Avenue, and I need to go to the bathroom. After all the things I have heard from Randy and Brian, I am almost afraid to use the men's room at Bloomingdale's. I'm sure I'll feel self-conscious or embarrassed, as if I were in a gay bar with the lights on. As it is, I don't even like going shopping there. The sales people all wear expensive clothes and cologne, and they have such neatly trimmed hair and polished shoes. They act as if they are really too good to be selling things. And so everyone who shops there gets all dressed up in their best clothes and cologne and acts as if they are really too good to be buying things. I'm sure the bathrooms are jammed with expensively dressed men waiting to have sex in the stalls. But it is a long walk home and I really need to go, so I walk into the store and take the escalator to the seventh floor.

NO LOITERING

says a sign, written in large white letters on a red background. Beneath it, another signs says

"These premises are monitored periodically by security staff."

I know that they aren't kidding. A friend of Brian's was caught having sex there. They treated him like a criminal, escorting him through the store in handcuffs. The only reason they didn't arrest him was because he agreed not to even shop at Bloomingdale's for seven years. It's scary to think that people can be arrested for having sex. It wasn't as if anyone was hurting anyone else. I suppose Bloomingdale's doesn't like the idea of men having sex in their bathrooms.

As I walk in the door, a man is facing me with his fly open. He is tall, attractive, tan, with silver curly hair, and he is wearing a red sweater, dark pants, and a trench coat. I can't figure out why his fly is open unless he has just finished relieving himself and is about to zip up. I walk past him to the urinal, and he steps up to the one next to me.

I feel my embarrassment growing as I unbutton the fly of my jeans and pull myself out of my underwear. Amazingly enough, I am able to go without any discomfort or delay. I look down at myself, never glancing up to see if the man next to me is looking. When I am finished, I walk to the sink to wash my hands. I look at myself in the mirror and wonder why anyone at Bloomingdale's would want to have sex with me when I haven't shaved and my hair is too long. As I am leaving, I glance at a pair of feet in a stall. They are dressed in expensive Italian loafers. I wonder if they are waiting for someone.

Taking the escalator down, I imagine the attractive man at the urinal following me out onto the street, where I will tell him that I'm not interested, and besides, hasn't he heard of AIDS? But that wouldn't be very nice, and besides, maybe he only wanted to fool around safely. I could just smile and tell him sorry, you've got the wrong guy. I am almost disappointed that he doesn't appear from behind me as I leave the store.

As much as I hate to admit it, I have to say that, for a second, it was exciting, thinking of what might happen, feeling attractive and desirable. Sensing the urgency of someone else's need, and realizing that I could have enjoyed myself with him, if I wanted to. But I know that afterwards, I would feel strange, disconnected from myself. It takes so long to understand sex. And it is so hard to remember that what is right for me may not be right for somebody else.

"WHO'S THE POSTCARD FROM?"

I am trying to speak in my most disinterested voice. Green, blue, brown, trees, grass, and some kind of building. A lodge? A resort? And that handwriting which I can already recognize.

"Oh, a friend. His name is Jeff Joseph."

My face is talking to Daniel again, saying something I'd rather he didn't hear. I dampen a piece of paper toweling beneath the faucet of his kitchen sink, and wipe up an orange ring of juice from the kitchen table.

"Don't worry. I'm not interested in him. Sexually," he says. He shows me the back of the postcard.

Dear D.,

What am I to do? Since October, I've not been the same. I still hope for something, some kind word, minutes of your time, an afternoon. My family is beginning to suspect something. They notice that I've changed. I am not at all myself, I trip into things. Yesterday, I broke a vase. What can it mean?

> J.J.

P.S. Stocks in the diamond mine continue to rise.

"Where did you meet him?"

"In passing."

In passing. I bend my head lower over the table, scrub a small brown stain. Probably coffee. All right, I won't ask you again where you met him. Not yet.

"He's got a crush on me, I think. He's very lonely. His family has money. They don't know he's gay. They've got him right under their thumbs."

"Poor guy."

I pull a chair away from the table, checking the green oilcloth seat for crumbs.

THREE POSTCARDS. And I have deliberately never sent him anything, card or letter. Andrea would say it was too intense, to send letters to someone you were dating. Andrea would say it might frighten him off, to mail him postcards.

This time, the Blue Lady's fingers feel just like jealousy. Poking around inside my chest. But the pain is different, almost worse. Her hands touch the old places, the scars, Michael and his lover, betrayal, and,

But he said he wasn't interested in him, "sexually." But I can tell by the tone of his voice when he speaks of this Jeff Joseph that he is more than just "a friend." And how would someone with a diamond mine meet Daniel "in passing"?

This is not a contest. You can't convince someone to love you. I can only be me. He told me he loves me. I believe him. If he chooses to spend time with this person, what are you going to do? He has a right to have friends. He has a right to his privacy.

And if you found out they were sleeping together? Monogamy, fidelity. You have no agreement. You never asked for either one. Maybe this time I should've asked. Maybe this time, it's too late instead of too soon.

And even if you found out he was fucking this man, what then? You know you wouldn't leave Daniel. Not over this. Is your heart so small that it won't allow him to love other people? The only important thing, the thing that really matters, is what takes place between the two of you. You told him so yourself. As long as the two of you talk things over, you can work it out.

But what if he's afraid to talk? Three postcards from this man, and yet he has never mentioned him to me. Until now. And if I wouldn't have asked, I might never have heard a word about him.

I am not a saint. I am not perfect. I don't know if I can love someone who also loves somebody else. Sometimes, I would do anything to rid myself of the

Blue Lady's hands, to feel no more pressure on my chest, no fingers moving in and out of me. If love is always pain, then maybe Randy is right. Maybe I really want to be alone. I can leave him, if I want. I am not

Wait. The hardest thing. But I will wait.

"EXCUSE ME. Zeta Beta Tau?"

He is blond, probably about twenty or so, with a round face, and pimples. He wears a thin leather tie, and at first I'm not sure if he's speaking to me. Then I remember. I am wearing Daniel's old fraternity sweatshirt, from when he was in undergraduate school.

No, the sweatshirt isn't mine. It belongs to someone older, someone no longer a student.

"Would you be interested in joining?" He invites me to something. A rush party? I don't know anything about fraternities. No thanks, I'm not a student.

I want to tell him that the sweatshirt belongs to my lover. I would like him to know that one of his fraternity brothers is gay. But instead, I thank him for the invitation, and continue walking through the library.

I AM READING a gay newspaper. Even though most of the stories are about AIDS or politics, there is always a photograph of a half-naked man on the front page.

The first thing I read is from an interview with someone about how AIDS has affected his life.

"I keep wondering what will happen, when the AIDS epidemic starts to infect more straight people. Already there has been an increase in violence against gay people. I wonder where I will be safe. Part of me wants to escape with my lover to some private corner of the world. But another part of me thinks we would be safer here in New York—safety in numbers, and all that. Plus I feel a responsibility to be here for my gay and lesbian brothers and sisters. I guess we will probably all hang together."

Daniel continues to kiss me in the street, even though I warn him about what might happen if some creep sees us. I am really torn by the whole thing. Andrea says if you act ashamed, or as if you are afraid, you will begin to feel those things. I don't want to feel ashamed of my love for Daniel. But I also don't want either one of us to be hurt. Sometimes, I think the whole AIDS thing is just a terrible dream. It seems so strange, that we should be born at this particular time in history. Just when things were really starting to change, when gay people were beginning to feel free to live their lives openly and honestly, this horrible disease occurs. And I fall in love with someone. Maybe it has always been like this. Maybe something has always existed to keep us fighting for our lives, fighting to be ourselves. Maybe it is another test, a way of making us stronger. Or maybe it is just another disease, like syphilis before penicillin. Maybe it is just a coincidence that it affected gay men first.

Next, I read an interview with a gay candidate for political office.

"We really don't know who we are anymore. In reaction to the 1950s stereotype of the swishing, lisping, bitchy faggot, there has been a wholesale rejection of the (culturally defined) 'feminine' in us. Butch is 'in' with a vengeance. Everyone belongs to a gym. The gay male media is obsessed with the fetishization of the male body. There is now even a sign in The Spur (a West Village gay bar) reading 'No Cologne Please.' The complaint is voiced that because of AIDS, gay men have had to adopt 'straight' values— presumably monogamous sexual relationships, casual dating and socializing, the elimination of anonymous sex—values which are often cited as being in some way responsible for the oppression of gays. But are these values really (culturally defined as) 'straight'? Aren't they in fact values which have been traditionally defined as 'feminine'? It seems to me that what gay men have done is to co-opt a straight view of masculinity, to identify and in some sense align themselves with a certain kind of straight man, a repressed, femophobic, commitment fearing, insensitive, Marlboro cigarette-ad-type man. A tragic move, considering the realities of the political situation."

I wonder what Randy and Brian would have to

say about that. They aren't very political. Brian never marches in the Gay Pride Parade. And he doesn't even like to be seen outside of a gay bar. He and Randy always vote Republican.

Here is something I will show Daniel. It is about his club. Actually, I better not show him, or he might think I am trying to discourage him from going.

"The success of the jerk-off club depends on a kind of duality, a contradiction which must remain hidden in order for the club to continue to function successfully. On the one hand, group activity is stressed and encouraged. The club's erotic environment depends on the willingness of its members to participate in scenes of mutual masturbation, to treat fellow members considerately, and to avoid alienating less desirable members. There is a kind of 'do unto others' mentality, which stresses brotherhood, community, and group (as opposed to coupled) sexual encounters. To offer an example, a recent newsletter of The Club's stresses the importance of treating those members with whom one chooses not to participate kindly and with consideration. 'Be polite. No one likes to be rejected, so let him down easy. And remember, we're all here for some hot group action.'

"On the other hand, part of the club's eroticism depends on a de-personalization of the sexual 'object.' For some men, the club is exciting because it is a 'safe' way to act out risky behavior. It simulates sex before AIDS, casual, anonymous, abundant sex.

Thus fellow club members are sometimes designated as so many 'dicks,' 'studs,' or some other term which emphasizes the object quality of the sexual partner at the expense of his personhood. Again, to offer an example from a newsletter, The Club charges 'five dollars per dick' for entry into its facilities, and features 'plenty of lube, beer, and all the cock you can pull.'"

I have to admit that Daniel's club's newsletter bothers me. I can understand some men enjoying a jerk-off club. But all that stuff about "pulling dicks" and "pounding puds." It reminds me of little boys talking about sex, laughing while they look at their father's "dirty" magazines behind the family barn. It is so "male" in a way I just don't understand, such a denial of the emotions involved in sex.

Sometimes I think the real sexual differences are between men and women rather than between straight and gay people. Can you imagine a lesbian jerk-off club? "Bye honey, I'm off to the Clit Club!" Maybe part of being a man is feeling differently about sex from women. But where does that leave someone like me, except still feeling like an outsider?

THERE IS ONE THING common to all the men I've ever loved, from the time I was a child until now. It isn't the shape of their mouths. It isn't even the fact of their tears, the tears I have only seen when we were in bed together. And it has nothing at all to do with needing to be saved, or feeling desperate or lonely.

Daniel. Michael. Even Brian. Maybe even my father. The thread that connects them all is their pain, that terrible pain of being a man. That need for tenderness, that need to love and be loved, the need that must never be revealed. Because of the shame. Because of the fear. For all of these men, being a man means never revealing their need to be loved, their need to love someone in return.

All of them fight to keep it inside, their need to be gentle, to hold someone's hand, to lay their heads on someone's chest. They cover it over, they hide it behind their jerk-off clubs, or anonymous sex, or saving someone else's life, or helping someone else. But still it is there, no matter how they may deny it, it is always there, waiting, inside them.

I can see it. I know these men. Whenever I meet them, I can feel the tenderness deep inside them. That is the Blue Lady's gift to me, her fingers in my heart, her words, "How much room?" I meet these men, and I know. I know that loving them will be painful and difficult. I know that they will probably not be able to love me the way I once thought I needed to be loved, recklessly, generously. They are almost never the kind of men who say "I love you" for no reason at all. But I also know that these men need me. I know that for them, my love is not poison. It is the one gift I can give them.

In some ways, they are my opposite. My love rushes out ahead of me. It doesn't know how to hide itself. It doesn't know how to be silent. But Andrea has taught me to temper my love, to be quiet, relax, take my time. She has taught me how to love the kind of man the Blue Lady brings to me.

It is this hidden tenderness, and the pain, that has led me to love other men. And when they love me, when they finally allow themselves to take the gift I bring them, then I know I can die. I know that my life has not been wasted, that I am not bad. I know that I can face dying, knowing that I've loved someone.

But loving men is the easy part; it is staying with them that is difficult. I love them for what I see inside them. But I stay with them for other reasons, the way they treat me, the kindness they show me when we're together.

I know I love Daniel. There is no doubt in my mind about it. But can I stay with him?

"A MEMBER OF MY CLUB asked me to be in a movie."

"What kind of movie?"

"A porno movie. I'd be jerking off. But no one would know it was me. I'd be wearing a leather mask."

A leather mask. Like the one they found covering the face of that model, shot in the back of the head, and his body burned. In the woods, they found him.

"I assume it would be only 'safe sex' in this movie."

"Of course."

What can I say, how do I react, what are the right words?

"Why would you want to cover your face with a leather mask? It's the prettiest part of you."

I kiss him on the forehead.

HOW MUST the Blue Lady have felt that night, when her baby first moved inside her? It was probably something like what I feel when her fingers move in me, the pain that is almost too awful and yet somehow sweet, almost reassuring. The reminder that love is so very hard to bear. I don't know. After a while, the words run out, the stories I tell myself don't quite seem to fit the feeling anymore. I mean, there is really no way to describe how it feels. That place where there are no words, that time when there is only hugging yourself. That is what the Blue Lady must have felt that night, when her baby first kicked. Fear and happiness and everything at once, the terror and sadness and wonderment. That must be how it feels, to have a baby inside you. And for her, it was probably worse, knowing how much pain was to come for both of them.

When Michael was away at school, I sometimes fantasized about having a baby. I never told anyone about it, except for Jerry. Jerry was directing a show I was in. He knew about Michael, but he didn't care; he was always coming on to me, behind the set, in the dressing rooms. He would slip his hand between my legs as I waited in the wings for my cue. Once he even grabbed my ass in front of the whole cast. I pushed his hands away from me, and told him to knock it off. He just laughed and did it again. He was fifteen years older than me. I guess I could not have minded it too much, or I would have left the show.

The night that I told him, we were sitting in an Italian restaurant, one of those places with white linen tablecloths, and red glass candles covered in white plastic netting. I remember the smell of garlic on his breath, and the tone of his voice as he told me what he thought of me, how I was sick.

I was lonely. I missed Michael, and I was thinking of what it would be like, to have a baby. Not to father one; to feel one moving inside me, to know that in nine months, a person would come out of me, a person who might one day be a sculptor or poet or dancer, someone with tiny hands and soft hair and breath that was warm and smelled indescribably sweet. And it would live inside me, feeling safe and comfortable, talking to me in its silent baby voice whenever it felt lonely, or knew I was feeling a little depressed. I would take such good care of my baby, protecting it from cigarette smoke and alcohol and falls down the stairs. And then the real miracle would happen, it would come out of me, alive, crying, waiting for me to pick it up and hold it tight, tight against me, as tight as my arms could stand it. It must be the most amazing thing in the world, to bear a child. A real miracle. And that was what I wanted someday; to bear a child, Michael's child.

"You're sick. You really want to be a woman, don't you? You think having a baby would make things better between you and Michael? Jesus Christ, you're like some teenage girl trying to saddle some jerk into marrying her. You really need help."

Jerry pointed his bread at me as he talked. The garlic on his breath was making me dizzy, and his voice was so loud I thought the whole restaurant would hear. But I knew I wasn't sick. I didn't want to be a woman; I wanted to be a man having a child. Maybe my timing wasn't so great; things were pretty lousy between Michael and me. And maybe I was forgetting the bad things, the sickness in the mornings, and your body all swelled up and strange. But I wasn't sick, just because I wanted to have a child.

Thank God I didn't, I wasn't able, to have his baby. What would I do today, with a child to support, and Michael off somewhere with somebody else? I would really be in trouble then.

I try not to think about Daniel's baby. Besides the fact that it would be impossible, it is much too soon to even start imagining his mouth and my hands and his eyes on another little person. Even if one of us wanted to father a child, we would have to worry about whether or not we might be unknowingly exposed to the AIDS virus. But still, sometimes, I wonder what it would be like, to feel another person inside me, sleeping, waiting to be born. It must be indescribable.

DANIEL LIES ON HIS STOMACH, his face turned left, resting on the pillow, he shows me his mouth, the pleasure I see in his mouth, I kiss his mouth, I am on top of him, pressing my chest against his back, moving my cock between his legs, touching his balls, they are soft, soft as the feathers of a baby bird, I kiss his neck, I touch his ass, I move between his legs, I press my cock against

The telephone rings.

"Don't answer that."

But it may be his parents, his father is sick. I roll over onto my back. He answers the phone.

"Hello."

It is not his father. But I don't bother to ask who it is. I can tell from the sound of Daniel's voice.

Jeff Joseph.

Two, three, four times a day this man calls whenever I am at Daniel's apartment. I am afraid my face is talking again, voicing my displeasure. I get up out of bed, wash my hands.

Don't let him see that you're upset. Jealousy is ugly, and you have nothing to be jealous about. He can have his friends, he is allowed to have friends.

I sit at the kitchen table, turning the triangular shape of the empty napkin holder over in my hands. Several minutes, he is on the phone. I don't listen, I don't want to hear, I act as if I trust him.

"It was Jeff Joseph again. I don't know why he calls so often."

"Why don't you ask him to stop?"

"I have."

I am thinking of Andrea, thinking of what she would say, how she would tell me to act. Don't be hostile; be calm. Tell him exactly what is bothering you. But don't accuse him of anything.

"I don't mind that he calls so often, except that it interrupts our time together. Look at what just happened. He has effectively put a stop to what we were doing."

Good. Andrea would congratulate you on your choice of words.

"But we've already made love once this morning."

Once? Is that my quota for the day? Don't be angry. He can see the anger in your face.

"I know he calls a lot, but he's lonely. His family doesn't understand him."

I am tired of this Jeff Joseph person, tired of his postcards, his money, his family problems. I wonder

"Where did you meet him?"

"In passing."

"Where was 'in passing'?"

"A movie theater." He looks away from me. He stands at the kitchen sink, naked, washing his hands. "It was back in October."

A movie theater. I don't need to ask what kind of movie theater. I can guess by the look on his face, the look which he will not let me see. I imagine him in the dark with his pants open. I imagine the row of seats, the light of the screen, I imagine him reaching over into the lap of someone else. Her fingers find the soft spot quickly.

But that was back in October. Before he gave me the ring. Before I told him I loved him. Before he told me the same.

"He says I'm his best friend. He's a very lonely guy."

"Poor man."

"And he has more money than he knows what to do with."

I know. I've seen the presents around Daniel's apartment, the books, the cologne, the things I can't possibly afford to give him.

"He wants me to go away with him for a weekend. To a resort in Vermont."

The postcard—green, blue, brown, trees, a house? A resort.

"What did you tell him?"

"I'll think about it. I might like to go."

YOU LOUSY BASTARD. All the months I waited, took my time, all the months I kept calm. All the time I trusted you. And now, someone with money shakes his dick in your face and you're ready to dump me. I didn't send you letters and postcards; Andrea said it might scare you off. I didn't give you presents; Andrea said that would be too intense for you. Obviously, she was wrong.

Today, this morning, I feel nothing, no Blue Lady's hands. I made her up, and I can just as easily destroy her. I push her fingers away from me, I don't want her poking her claws into me today. She makes me sick with her pompous voice, and her question. I am not a saint. I am not perfect. Maybe I am bad, maybe I caused this. All this time, he's been laughing at me, sneaking around behind my back, pulling his dick with strangers. I trusted him. I believed he was still that dark boy in the photograph, I believed he was gentle. But all the while, he was laughing at me. It is just like Michael all over again, Michael and his "other" lover.

I can leave you. I am not desperate, there are other men, men who don't belong to jerk-off clubs, men who would be faithful to me without my having to ask, men who would love me. I am attractive, I am a good person, you are not the only man. I don't have to share you with other people because I am lucky to be loved at all.

But I don't say any of these things.

I need time to think about this. My heart is not small. But is it big enough for this? I love Daniel. Whether I like it or not, I am already in love with him. I can't throw away these past few months unless I am sure about this. Maybe I'm wrong. Maybe I can live with this. Maybe I can't.

"You know that nothing matters to me except what happens between the two of us. As long as we talk about things," I say.

"I *do* talk about things. I've told you about him before."

"But only when I started asking questions first."

I WONDER if he would have ever told me how they'd met, if I hadn't asked him first.

"But sometimes, people do things they're ashamed of."

What else have you done, that you haven't told me? I want to trust you. I want to be able to trust you.

Are they sleeping together? He said he wasn't interested in him. Sexually. But that doesn't mean they might not still be having sex. Look at how they met. And he's made no promises to you. Monogamy. Fidelity. You have no agreement.

He would tell me, if I asked him. I know he would. But I don't think I can bring myself to ask.

His face, when he's asleep, Oh God, he is such a child. A movie theater. I will never understand.

RANDY AND I are sitting in the oversized seats of a chartered bus. We are riding to Queens, to a warehouse sale, to choose a mattress for Randy and Brian's new bed. We are surrounded by gray-haired women with shopping bags. I tell Randy about Jeff Joseph, the presents, the postcards, the phone calls.

"Someone will always be trying to break the two of you up."

We leave the bus, and walk into the warehouse. It reminds me of a barn with a linoleum floor. We walk across the room, past the dishwashers, the mirrors, the piles of sheets and towels, over to the mattresses.

"Someone is always going to be pursuing one or both of you. It happens to Brian and me all the time. Help me look for extra-firm."

We take turns testing the mattresses. They are stacked upright in a wooden frame that allows us to move between them. Together, we lean up against one, as if we are sleeping standing up.

"Do you think I get hysterical over every postcard or gift that Brian gets from some old trick? Daniel loves you. He's not really interested in this other guy." He smiles at me.

"But what about Vermont, what if he goes away for the weekend with this guy?"

"Then you can break up with him," he says, no longer smiling.

DO I ASK HIM to choose between the two of us? I could ask him. I think he would probably choose me. But I won't be that kind of person. I won't tell him how to behave, I won't tell him who he may spend his time with. And besides, he'd probably resent me for forcing him to choose. I can't be that kind of person.

But if he is dating both of us, don't I have the right to know? I can stand almost anything but the feeling of being laughed at. And nothing is more frightening than not knowing. If I knew either way, then I would know what to do. I know about the club, and it doesn't bother me. Too much.

But I can't bring myself to ask him if they sleep

together. If they don't, I would look like a fool, and he might resent the fact that I asked. And if they do sleep together, I don't know how I would feel.

Wait. I will wait. It is so hard sometimes, to wait.

"SO, HOW ARE THINGS GOING?" she asks.

Lousy. The story of Jeff Joseph spills out of my mouth—the postcards, the telephone calls, the gifts, the movie theater. And now this trip to Vermont.

Andrea removes her glasses, and sets them down on the pink marble coffee table.

"I know that this has hurt you. But you said yourself they met back in October."

October. Months ago. Before. But at a movie theater. I imagine it over and over again, the dark theater, his pants open, the musty smell, it makes me sick, it frightens me.

"I think it was Oscar Wilde who said, 'Nothing human disgusts me.'"

I am not disgusted. I'm angry. I'm hurt. If he wouldn't go prowling around places like porno theaters, this kind of thing wouldn't happen. And when did it happen, what night in October? Or was it during the day? And afterwards, did they talk, meet for lunch, have dinner somewhere? How did he get Daniel's telephone number, why did he give it to him? What was wrong with me? How was I not good enough? What should I have done instead?

"What happened with Jeff probably has nothing

at all to do with you. You know that. Haven't you done things that you've later regretted? What about that man with the yacht?"

I spent a weekend on a yacht once, getting stoned and having sex. He was a Vietnam vet who smoked cigars, he was big and burly, with a black moustache. His arm had been blown off in the war. I could see the wires beneath his skin where it had been reattached. He told me he wanted to marry me at sea. He told me that just thinking about me made his tongue hard. Poppers, marijuana, cocaine, and some of the best sex I'd ever had in my life. But then the weekend was over and I realized that we had nothing to say to each other. He called me several times, but I never saw him again.

"Sure, I've done things I've regretted. But not while I was seeing someone else. And besides, it's happened maybe once or twice. Daniel has made a career out of it."

"What do you want? Do you want to break up with Daniel?"

No. I don't think so. I want to trust him. I want to believe him. I want to believe that he loves me.

"Do you think Jeff Joseph wears a ring from Daniel?"

I look down at my finger, the gold band, the gift.

No.

"Do you think Jeff has keys to his apartment?"

No. Of course not. We would probably have bumped into each other, if

"Do you think Daniel introduces Jeff to his friends as his lover?"

No. What would they think, how could he explain, having two lovers.

"Do you think Daniel has told his father about Jeff?"

No, the man is sick, he would never understand, especially after Daniel has already told him about me. And besides, I remember . . .

"So, what's the problem? Daniel is acting as if he loves you. He even tells you so. What more do you want?"

I know it isn't rational, what I am feeling. But I feel betrayed. I trusted him. What if they are sleeping together?

"Look, there are more important things than sexual fidelity. As long as the two of you continue to talk these things over, then the intimacy between you will grow. And that is what matters most.

"You can break up with him, if you like. You have the right to choose someone who will be faithful to you. If that is what you really want. But there will always be something, some problem that the two of you will have to work out together. If not fidelity, then something else. It's never going to be perfect."

But it isn't fair. If he wants Jeff, he should be with him. I'm not forcing anybody to do anything. I haven't tricked him into loving me.

"You're right, it isn't fair to you. Ideally, Daniel

shouldn't see this man. He is having a relationship with you. But things aren't always fair.

"I don't think he's sleeping with this other man. He probably just enjoys the attention. Look, you and Daniel spend four nights together a week. Do you really think he's spending the other three with someone else?"

But what about Vermont? What if he decides to go away with Jeff for a weekend?

But I already know how Andrea will answer.

"As hard as it will be for you, I think you should let him go."

I know. I've already decided that if he wants to go, I will not make a scene. I won't force him to choose me. I won't threaten him. If he really wants to go, then that is what I want for him. Even if it means a weekend of playing cards with the Blue Lady's hands.

"Sometimes, people need to test their relationships. They don't do it deliberately, consciously. He probably just wants to see how you'll react. He wants to know if you will be the kind of person to tie him down, to tell him what he can and can't do."

Typical male fear of relationships, fear of being swallowed up, fear of disappearing. But I'm a man. Why don't I feel that fear?

"Okay," she says. That is my cue, the hour is over. I reach in my pocket for the money.

I AM LYING IN DANIEL'S BED, alone. He has left for an

audition. I hate being alone in this apartment. It reminds me of that night, the jerk-off party, waiting for him to return.

Jeff Joseph. No matter what Randy says, no matter what Andrea says, I can't seem to shake my fear that I will lose him to this man. He never talks about him unless I bring him up.

"Sometimes, people do things . . ."

What are you not telling me? Trust him. Behave as if you trust him, and you will feel as if you trust him. I want to trust him.

He will be gone for at least a few hours. His drawers. Maybe if I looked through his drawers, I would find the letters from Jeff. Then I would know what was really happening between the two of them.

No. I will not be that kind of person. I will not be turned into that kind of person by my own jealousy.

But maybe the letters will convince me once and for all that they are not sleeping together. Maybe the letters . . .

No. Andrea would say no. Get up out of bed and take a shower. If you act as if you don't trust him

I open a drawer. Towels, orange, green, nothing hidden in the bottom. Another drawer, white socks, underwear, T-shirts. Another drawer, papers, I recognize the handwriting, the postcards

Shut the drawer. Don't read them. It will only make you feel terrible, it will only frighten you more. It

Just this one. I'll read just this one letter.

Peaches melba, diamond mine, all the stupid usual things, October, Jesus, he's practically engraved on his forehead the day he and Daniel jerked off in that movie theater. I need you, what would I do without you, what can I possibly have with you, that morning, we toasted with grapefruit juice, I walked home in the rain, I'll try not to call so much, I'll

Morning. Toasted with grapefruit juice. What was he doing at Daniel's in the morning? They spent the night together. In this bedroom. In this bed. They are sleeping together.

No. Daniel told you, Jeff has money, no job, no regular hours. Maybe he came over in the morning. They aren't sleeping together. No one is laughing at you.

Andrea was right, now look what you've done. What are you going to tell Daniel?

"I happened to be looking through your drawers and I came across this letter from Jeff Joseph. Are you fucking him?"

Now you will pay for this. You behaved as if you didn't trust him. And now all you can do is live with the doubt. You can never tell him about this, never ask about this letter.

The Blue Lady takes her revenge, I roll over onto my stomach, hold myself until the pain passes, hold my hands up against my chest.

JEALOUSY

I am no sinner.

Whatever I take
I have earned,
nights of gathering up
the unraveled threads
of your sleep, nights
you pressed me
face down
deep into the earth,
split me open
like a seed.

I dream a poison
to serve you for supper,
make your mouth forget
the taste of those hundreds
whose bodies have traveled
beneath your tongue.
I would come to you
like a child, hands
hidden behind my back,
I would play in your lap,
pretend in your pockets.

Then slip the bitter pill
between your lips
and watch you suffer.

Leave my home.

My back is not a bench
on which you can waste
your afternoons.

Flash your treasures
at someone else,
someone rich,
who never imagines murder.

I have no excuse
for my awkward arms
catching your words in the air,
for my body
blooming purple
beneath your hands,
like some grotesque
and waxy flower.

WE ARE IN BED, Daniel and I, the covers pulled up around our shoulders. He is talking to me, telling me about Jeff Joseph. That is the joke I play on myself. I ask him to tell me about this man. And then I complain that my life is too full of him.

"He says I'm the best thing that ever happened to him."

I could say those words to you. I could tell you the truth, that I've never loved anyone the way I love you. But Andrea would say that was too intense. She would say that I might scare you off, saying those kinds of things to you. Maybe she is right. You are here with me tonight, and not with him.

"He says I saved his life."

Is that what you want, Daniel? Someone to save, an empty pitcher waiting to be filled with you? Have I been wrong all these months, taking my time, keeping my distance from you, showing you that I am a whole person, that I am not desperate or afraid? I tell you that you are beautiful, and that you make me laugh. I tell you that you are one of the gentlest men I have ever known. I tell you that I love you.

But I cannot be saved. Not by you, not by anybody. I must be able to save myself. Maybe years ago, maybe when I was seventeen, I might have been able to let some man save me. But I doubt it. No matter what I may have told myself, no matter what I may have thought about my parents, about how my life was going to be just like theirs. Except that I was gay. Except that I love men. No matter what I may have said in the past, I don't think I would have ever allowed some man to save my life. I am not my mother. I have never been my mother.

But I need you, Daniel. I want you to be part of my life. Maybe I can't need you the way he, Jeff Joseph, needs you. But I do need you. You have taught me how to love someone. You have given me that gift, the gift of the Blue Lady's hands. My life will never be the same, no matter what may happen to us, no matter who may come between us. I am so grateful for having met you.

But once again, I say none of these things. It is still too soon. There will be time enough to say these things, and so much more. But not now.

"I love you," I say, and kiss his forehead. I lay on my stomach, reaching my arm across his chest. I am not afraid.

IT IS MORNING. Daniel has gone out to buy some milk and a newspaper, and I am left alone in this apartment, this Pandora's box of an apartment, where every door and cupboard and closet waits for me to give in to this maddening curiosity. I imagine the letters, postcards, photographs, whispering their secrets, I hear their voices, but I can't make out the words. I hear them laughing at me, knowing it is only a matter of time before my resolve breaks, and I run to the dresser, rummage through his clothes, empty the drawers of his socks and underwear, tear open the pillows, check beneath the mattress. Maybe Jeff Joseph himself, or some stray member of Daniel's club, is waiting behind a door, waiting for me to leave so that he might slip into my seat at the table, my place in bed beside him.

I don't want to behave like this. I want to trust Daniel, to believe the things he tells me. But what about the things he doesn't tell me? I say to myself that I am only looking for some small reassurance, some final evidence that will convince me one way or another of how he feels about me. But Andrea says I'm kidding myself. She thinks that as long as I continue to act as if I don't trust him, the feelings will build and build, no matter what kind of "evidence" I ultimately discover, until eventually I will be reduced to searching his pockets, listening in on his telephone conversations, steaming open his mail.

It is horrible, to feel this way. It reminds me of being a child, stumbling across the crushed and decaying body of a tiny bird, a baby fallen from the nest, its neck broken, its downy feathers stained with blue-green flies, and I cover my eyes, I turn away, but I can't help taking a second look, and another, there is part of me that would spend an afternoon staring at this secret rotting in the grass at the foot of a tree, if I didn't force myself to hurry away.

I've got to keep busy. As long as I am active, I can prevent myself from doing the things I know I will later regret. I could make breakfast, except that the refrigerator is almost empty. Maybe I'll take a shower while he's gone, and then when he returns, we can go somewhere to eat.

The telephone rings.

I wonder what I should do. Maybe I should just let it alone. Whoever it is will call back later. But what if Daniel's father has suddenly gotten worse, what if his mother is calling him to tell him to come to the hospital right away, before it's too late? Or what if it is Daniel himself, asking me to meet him somewhere for breakfast? The worst that could happen is that it could be someone who part of me wants to speak to anyway, the secrets in the box, the bird in the grass. Better to know than to wonder, better to see and be sure than to imagine.

"Hello?"

"Uh, Daniel? Is this Daniel?" The voice is a man's, slightly nasal, and the words are spoken rapidly, disjointedly, there is a jittery rhythm to the sentences, as if each word were being pushed out of his throat, one at a time.

"No, he's not here right now. May I take a message, please?" I sound like a child who has learned from his mother the proper way to answer the phone when she's away.

"Oh. Could . . . is it possible that he'll be home soon?"

"He just stepped out for a few minutes. He should be back at any moment."

"Oh. I guess I'll call back later. Thank you."

"May I tell him who called?" There's a harshness in my voice as I say the words quickly, before he has a chance to hang up. I imagine I know who it is, who would possibly hesitate to leave his name.

"Oh, just a friend. Jeff Joseph is my name."

I wonder if I am supposed to react to the sound of his name. Quickly, I think, tell him all the things you've been thinking, the words you've rehearsed in your head, "Stay away from Daniel, stop calling us, find your own lover, I'm sure the porno theaters of New York are filled with men who'd endure your charms, who'd be only too anxious to receive your school-girl notes, your generous gifts." But how would I ever explain it to Daniel, how would I ever convince him that I could be trusted alone in his apartment again, that I was not a shrew or a fishwife, or some sort of horrible person who would insult his friends, keep him in a noose, use my love like a leash. Besides, there is something almost pathetic in the sound of his voice, he speaks so quickly, I imagine him the kind of man who can't look in your eyes too long, whose hand trembles as he shakes yours. He told Daniel that he was his best friend, Daniel, whom he'd met one lonely afternoon in a movie theater. Now he is human. Now, it is almost possible to forgive him.

"I'll tell him you called. Good-bye." Quickly, I hang up the phone, put on my shoes, run to the bathroom to comb my hair. I've got to get out of this apartment before I go crazy. I am tired of the voices in my head, sick of the confusion, the questions. Why should I choose it to be this hard? There is nothing I owe him for loving me. I don't have to be grateful just for being with him.

I write a note, "Gone out for a while. I'll see you later, in time for dinner. Sorry I couldn't wait. Jeff Joseph called. I love you." I lock the door behind me.

I AM AT THE Museum of Modern Art, standing before a giant canvas of Jackson Pollock's.

I am thinking of Jeff Joseph, the letters. Why must Daniel save those damn letters? And why are they important enough to be saved in their own separate drawer? "The morning, walking home in the rain . . ."

I move closer to the painting.

One (#31, 1950). Gift of Sidney Janis.

I try to lose myself in the web of paint covering the canvas. I pretend I can crawl right into the picture, slip between the lines, and hide behind the blue drips, blue as clear as a sea on a sunny day. Blue as her robes.

Michael has blue eyes. He taught me about painting. He taught me how to recognize the different styles of all the Abstract Expressionists. It was a game. I would point to a canvas across the room and say "Rothko," or "De Kooning," or "Still." And for every painter I guessed correctly, he would squeeze my hand whenever a guard wasn't looking, or kiss me.

Michael and his "other" lover. At least I knew the truth. From the very first night I met him, I knew Michael had another lover. He never lied to me about that.

I move away from the painting, I step back out of the web of colors, the blue, the white, the black. I step back into the room.

"Excuse me."

"Oh God, I'm so sorry."

He has clear blue eyes, blue the color of water, the same blue I once saw in the eyes of a white tiger. His hair is brown, and he is about my age, slightly built, and his mouth is one of those mouths.

"Nice painting," he says with an accent. Southern?

"Do you like Pollock?"

"Never heard of him before," he laughs. He looks into my eyes for a moment, then looks away.

WE ARE EATING at the museum cafe. I spread my brie on the roll, try to avoid getting crumbs on the table.

"Where are you from?" I ask.

"Kentucky. I'm only in for a week or so. Just visiting." He pulls a green grape from the bunch in my basket, turns it over in his fingers. "Mind if I have one of these?" He pops it into his mouth.

"Go right ahead."

He touches my hand across the table.

"Why don't we go somewhere?"

"What do you mean?" I laugh. He takes a drink from my bottle of Perrier. Again, he looks into my eyes, then looks away.

He wants to have sex with me. Now, in the museum.

"Why don't you call me later this week?" I say. Monogamy. Fidelity. I have made no promises to anyone. "Maybe we can have dinner." Then, it will be all right to sleep with him. As long as you have dinner first, it won't be immoral, it won't be your first date with him.

"I will, I'll call you. But let's go somewhere now," he drawls.

"I'm sorry. I don't do that kind of thing." We get up from the table.

I follow him into the men's room.

"I just need to wash my hands," he says.

Once we are safely inside, he backs up against the wall. He kisses me hard on the mouth, puts his tongue inside my mouth.

"Don't."

"Oh, come on, you know you want it." He runs his hands over my chest, pinches my nipples through my shirt.

Maybe he's right. Maybe I do want it. Sex is a sport, meant to be enjoyed. I think of Randy and Brian. I think of Daniel and Jeff.

"Not here. Call me and we'll have dinner."

He rubs his hand on my cock, through my pants, he forces me up against the wall, presses himself into me. I feel the cold tile wall through my shirt, and feel myself getting hard. He kisses me again, I taste cigarette smoke on his breath, he reaches around me, grabs my ass.

"You've got a really nice butt," he says.

We hear the sound of footsteps outside the door. Quickly, we each duck into separate stalls. I hear the sound of someone taking a leak, then water running, the sound of the hand dryer blowing its hot air, footsteps. Then finally, the sound of the door shutting.

I open the door of my stall.

"Is it safe to come out?"

He opens the door. His cock is in his hands, he is stroking himself, looking at me.

Oh God, what do I do now, I don't want this, I don't.

He pushes me into the stall and closes the door behind him. What am I going to do? It's too late, I've let it go this far, maybe I do really want it, sex is a sport. I stand on the toilet seat, so only one pair of feet will show beneath the door of the stall. His cock is now level with my face.

Just get it over with, just open your mouth, use your hand, it doesn't matter, it doesn't mean anything, Daniel will never know, besides, what about Jeff, the movie theater, the jerk-off club, just get it over with, make him come and then rinse out your mouth, you'll never have to see him again, suck his dick and get it over with.

I open my mouth and he guides my head with his hands, down to his cock.

"EXCUSE ME."

"Oh God, I'm sorry."

He has clear blue eyes, blue the color of water, the same blue I once saw in the eyes of a white tiger. His hair is brown, and he is about my age, slightly built, and his mouth is one of those mouths.

"Nice painting," he says with an accent. Southern?

"Yes," I say, "One of my favorites here." I smile at him, and walk away.

I WILL NOT USE MY BODY as a weapon.

If I ever have sex with a stranger, it will be because I want to; not because of Jeff Joseph. I will not allow sex to become my weapon of revenge. My body is my own. Whatever happens between Daniel and me cannot change that.

I must decide. Either I confront Daniel about Jeff, tell him about the letters I've read, ask him if they are sleeping together. Or I forget the whole business, and get on with our relationship. I can't continue to torture myself like this, searching his drawers, peeking through the crack in his mailbox, looking for some evidence of infidelity. If I continue to act as if I don't trust him, there will be nothing left of our friendship. I really don't have a choice; I can't play policeman twenty-four hours every day.

And if I ask him, and if he tells me yes, sometimes they sleep together, what will I do? I know I won't leave him. As much as I'd like him to be faithful to me, I don't want it enough to demand it of him. I will not be that kind of person.

Besides, sexual fidelity is only one kind of fidelity. There are other, more important kinds.

In the morning sometimes, when we are both barely awake, he presses his face against mine, soft, it feels so soft and warm, he breathes into my face, and I drink it in, his air, the smell of him, I drink in his smell first thing that morning.

My heart is big enough. I have no need to feel ashamed.

I WONDER SOMETIMES what would happen, if my mother were to get sick again. At first I would probably blame myself. Then I would wonder how long it would be, before the same thing happened to me. But after all of that, after I had reminded myself that it couldn't possibly be my fault, and that nervous breakdowns are not contagious, then I guess I would probably just try and help her and my father and brothers to get through it. It is sad, that my first reactions to the news of her illness would probably be concern for myself. I suppose it is just a way of taking care of me. But it seems almost cruel.

It must be a terrible thing, to see your mother fall apart in front of you. Especially after everyone has told you how much you are just like her. I tried to imagine it once in a poem. I pretended my mother was sick again, and now it was my turn to take care of a child, the way my father had taken care of my brothers and me. I imagined that I had a baby sister, who needed me to help her make some sense out of the fact that her mother was gone for a while. I call the poem "While She Waits."

WHILE SHE WAITS

I won't let her touch you,
this cardboard woman
claiming to be our mother,
who hugs the empty pods of her breast
and drags disease behind her,
cat pulling its bloody prey.
Twice this witch has taken
the woman we adore.

First time, I was a baby.
Sparks of blue,
they burned the imposter away,
and Mom came back, contrite,
smiling like a saint.
We kissed her forehead,
praying the evil
was gone forever.

Twenty years, the terror is back,
my sister, I play parent,
teaching my fingers to smooth
your tangle of arms trapped in a sweater,
wiping away the watercolor
sadness staining your cheeks,
while our mother waits in Bedlam
for the hag to quit her skin.

"When will Mom come home?"
I plant in your memory
her woman's hands
preparing your meals
as if food were God come down,
brushing your blond hair to silk.

Not this madness of claws
scratching mortal sins in the air,
not this cipher
wrapped in your momma's robe,
haunting a hospital hall.

I don't blame my mother for what happened.
She couldn't help it, and she did the best she could
to try and get better. Even those terrible shock treatments. And now her illness is another one of those
stories that is with me forever.

WE ARE IN BED, Daniel and I. He is sleeping. I study
his face, remember the first time, his eyelashes, his
mouth, his eyes. Why are men so easy to love when
they are sleeping? It is as if sleep gathers together all

the tenderness inside them. It is as if all the secret
need flows into their faces. And they look just like
children.

Do I ask him about J.J.? No. It doesn't matter.
Maybe Daniel needs to love more than one man. It is
a good thing, to be able to love many people. Maybe
his heart is big enough to love many people. And
mine is big enough to let him.

"Good morning," he whispers, catching me staring at his face.

"Good morning."

I pull away the covers and lay on top of him.

"Ohhhh," he groans.

"I'm not that heavy," I laugh.

"No, you're not," he winces. I kiss his mouth
and roll off him.

He raises himself up on his hands, and looks
around his bedroom. The ashtray he made, the photograph of us together at Randy and Brian's on New
Year's Eve, the one card I sent him on our six month
anniversary, the photograph of his parents' wedding.

"This used to be my home," he says, turning to
me. "Now I guess it's ours."

There are no voices. Only the sound of me.

COULD I POSSIBLY have made up the whole story of
the Blue Lady? I don't know. No church has ever
told the story of her hands. And I am not Bernadette, not even a saint. But I believe in the Blue
Lady.

I don't know what will happen, with Daniel and me. I never ask about the future. Randy and Andrea both have taught me never to worry about the future. Relax, take your time, enjoy the time you have together.

Sometimes, I am still afraid. I don't understand, will never understand, the years of sex with strangers, the bathrooms, the bars. I am afraid that Daniel may one day do something he will be afraid to tell me. But I know that there is nothing he could tell me that would make me think less of him. And I can live with my fear, as long as I remember her hands.

The Blue Lady changes, and yet she is always the same. There is the pain. That never goes away. It just gets a little easier to live with. And it helps sometimes, to have a story that somehow makes it all make sense.

I press her hands against my chest, I hold them to me. Her fingers touch the rooms of my heart. I make no effort to pull myself free. "How much room?" she smiles at me. My heart is full of room. No matter how much pain I feel, there is always room enough inside me.

That is what it means, to love someone: to know the touch of the Blue Lady's hands.